BROKEN OBJECTS

PAUL MICHAEL PETERS

Sharleen-

Congratulations on winning the Library Thing give away. Thank you for supporting independent authors like me. I hope you enjoy this novel.

Paul Michael Peters

4/1/2023

PUBLISHED BY PAUL MICHAEL PETERS

QUOTES

"The world breaks everyone and afterward many are strong at the broken places. But those that will not break it kills. It kills the very good and the very gentle and the very brave impartially. If you are none of these you can be sure it will kill you too but there will be no special hurry."

— **Ernest Hemingway,**
A Farewell to Arms

"But if you fail to do this, you will be sinning against the Lord; and you may be sure that your sin will find you out."

Numbers 32:23

DEDICATION

For Kathryn Jean Erickson and all teachers who inspire reading.

SPECIAL THANKS

Krystyl Garrett, for her continued support and guidance throughout the writing of this novel.

Ivica Jandrijevic, for wonderful cover creations.

NOTE FROM THE AUTHOR

"Broken objects" in modern western culture is a concept based on the Japanese art of Kintsugi, the "golden journey," or Kintsukuroi, the "golden repair."

In practical terms, the artist repairs broken pottery by

mending it with a lacquer mixture that includes powdered gold, silver, or in some cases platinum. The artist rises above the nature of a repairman by doing this with a philosophical intent. A repairman hides the repair, attempting to return the object to its original state; the artist highlights the repair, showing the journey each object has taken, exposing the history the pottery carries that is greater than creation and usefulness.

It provides a connection and identification with things in this world that break, chip, and damage through its existence. In the home, these objects remind us that even the broken still have use and purpose, improving with time and care.

The following story is based on actual events. Names and locations have been changed for the safety and protection of people involved.

1861 - 1862

BOOK I

1861 - 1862

CHAPTER 1

"*N*ow, Linnea, you go with this man to the city."

She watched the thick mustache that tickled her face with each good night's kiss wiggle like a fuzzy spring caterpillar on every word. "Yes, Papa."

"He will take you to the factory. You will learn a trade." He looked at the man and tried his best at English, "What you call?"

"Bobbin carrier, sir."

The man removed his hat to hold respectfully at his waist, revealing a slick of greasy hair. "She will have the important job of carrying bobbins in the textile." Papa looked back to Linnea, his beloved daughter, and thought for a moment before his attempt at saying "bobbin carrier."

"It is an important role."

"How old is she, sir?"

Papa's face started to twist under the strain of the math as his fingers twitched in the count, "Ten."

"Oh, sir, that is the ideal age for a bobbin carrier, the best age in fact to send a girl to the factory. She will learn a trade and gain independence."

The flash of shame sending his beautiful daughter with this stranger took him for a moment. Finding it difficult to meet her big blue eyes, he instead looked at the soil beneath his feet, the dirt of the farm he cursed after the toil of these last years.

"Yes, Papa." Her blonde braids, tight from Mama taking out her anger at Papa in each elegant weave, a perfection of intricacy dangling past her shoulders. His gaze moved from the ground to the house window, where Mama's stony look hit him. Papa's eyes darted back to the safety of the cursed soil.

"Mr. Slater's textile will take very good care of your daughter," the man said to break the uncomfortable silence. "She will earn twenty-three dollars each month, of which ten will be sent here to you as long as she's in our employment."

Papa understood and nodded at the man's promise for her future.

"There are classes each night she can take to expand her education and a society in the city where she can meet people she might never encounter on the farm." The man reached into his jacket breast pocket to retrieve a billfold, "In fact, here are the first ten dollars, as a show of good faith."

Papa looked up from the ground, his eyes large at the ten-dollar bill. His stomach gave a gastronomic gurgle with the memory of the winter hunger. Mama and the four boys would be able to eat a real meal, but he would lose his only daughter. The horse would eat hay without mold, maybe a cup of oats to pull the plow deep, but Linnea would be absent from the table each night. Mostly, there would be no more kisses to the forehead before bed. The boys were too old for affection, and Mama distant. That warmth at night, knowing Linnea was safe, would be gone. This would be the smart move, the prudent choice, head over heart.

Papa took the ten-dollar bill. It was the largest single amount of money he had held at one time.

Papa's voice broke. "Linnea, time to go. Go now." He turned his back to go inside.

"Papa?"

The man firmly took Linnea by the wrist to pull her gently to the road, "Let us go to the coach, Linnea. Time for the deed to begin."

Linnea could hear the man talk. She did not understand all the words. He was in a hurry. His large steps were three times her stride. She had to run to keep pace. *What was the hurry on such a lovely day?*

When they passed the hedge, the house out of sight, she began to enjoy the trip to town as she had on Saturdays with Papa. In the spring, she would listen for the male Red-winged Blackbird, which Papa said brought good luck, its song, "conk-la-ree, conk-la-ree" a delight walking down the toe path. On this trip, it was absent. She did hear the "coooo-

OOOOO-woo-woo-woo" of the Mourning Dove. Everyone knew a visit from the Mourning Dove was a visit from a past relative. But she only knew Papa and Mama. She didn't have a Farfar. Perhaps this was good luck; it could be the Farfar she never knew was watching over her on this trip. Maybe Papa's Farfar was following her to town, "coooo-OOOOO-woo-woo-woo."

On reaching town, the man tightened his grip slightly. She wasn't wrong to think it was so that he wouldn't lose her, but for him, it was more to prevent her from running away. It had happened before. The money was exchanged, the agreement made, and the child would run home at the last moment, realizing what had transpired. This needed only happen once.

Instead of traveling by coach as he told her father they would, the two arrived at the US Postal Station where the Pontiac to Detroit train line ran. The coach would have been seventy-five cents and a three-day ride. Instead, the man bought a Penny Black stamp at the postal window and wrote down the address in care of R.F. Slater, Detroit. No one would be the wiser that he pocketed the difference in price. With a pin from his pocket, he attached the address to Linnea's shoulder, the stamp stuck to the paper.

The two walked through the station to the passenger entrance. On the station platform several older boys her brother's age dressed in dark blue trousers, jackets, and "kepi" caps. Three of them were fascinated by the green uniform one wore, making him stand out amongst the rest.

The man gave a slight tug on her arm drawing back her attention to the moment. On the far side of the platform they found the postal loading door where the white sacks of letters were ready to load.

Linnea found this site to be amazing. She had never been this close to a train before. Papa and her brothers spoke of when they had come to town to watch the trains when the station had opened in 1843. That was at least ten years before she was born. There were fireworks and cider that day. Pontiac was filled with people. Today seemed less fun but nearly as busy, exciting.

She watched as the man spoke with another, this one in uniform. He was much younger, similar in age to her oldest brother, Abell. This man seemed confused. The two continued to look down at her, and back at each other in exchanging words. After more words she didn't understand, the two shook hands. The man who gave Papa money took Linnea's wrist and placed it into the hand of the one in uniform.

THE WHITE CANVAS bag Linnea sat on was comfortable. She had a view of the farms that looked much like her home through the bars of the train car door. The sway from side to side kept the oil lamp on the ceiling hook swinging like a pendulum, "plick-clink," each time the metal connected to the wood roof.

Clickety-clack, clickety-clack, the train continued to roll forward. The plume of smoke always by its side smelled like the hen house when eggs went unrecovered for a week mixed with the hot tar Papa put on the roof four summers back. Clickety-clack, clickety-clack, plick-clink, plick-clink. Her favorite moments would arrive between the farms when children near her age would run to the train waving. This was fun. She and the brothers had done the same. To see she wasn't alone in this world made her smile. Standing on the white sack that was larger than she was, Linnea waved back with enthusiasm each time she saw the happy faces and waving hands of the children. It made her feel special as the train would pass and a moment of recognition changed the faces of some children from waving to pointing, as if to say, "There's a girl on that train. Look at her. Who is she?"

With the day's heat, the sulfur smell of rotten eggs and tar from the train became stronger. Linnea felt hot. She curled like a barn cat on the letter bag. Clickety-clack, plick-clink, became a soothing rhythm. The movement back and forth rocked her like a cradle into a deep, deep sleep.

ONLY OIL LAMP light from the roof hook reached her eyes as they opened. Gently the voice from the man in uniform stirred her from slumber. Linnea rubbed the crust from her eyes. She felt the need for a bath. Her white top was now gray and stiff from the smoke and dust of the day. The man in uniform encouraged her again to get up.

Something was different. The train had stopped. The door was open. She could only see his eyes looking up from outside. Both his hands extended from below to help her down to the ground as he softly encouraged Linnea to go to him with the motion to come. Standing and going to the door's edge, she could see a much larger world outside. This station was colossal compared to the one she had left that morning at home.

The man said something she understood, "End of the line."

Her eyes grew in size from the recognition, and gave him a smile. As she stepped forward, the man in the uniform helped her down. Past the darkness, a series of lights left her bewildered. She had only seen oil lamps before, but these lights were high atop poles in the air. The flame burned bright and barely flickered in the cool evening breeze behind the glass. She turned to the man who said a new phrase for her, "Gas lamps."

She tried to repeat the words aloud, which was returned by a chuckle from the man in the uniform. He reached into the train car, pulled the canvas bag to the edge of the door, and then, in one movement, got under the bag and placed it squarely on his shoulder. He offered his free hand to Linnea. She took it, and they walked together toward the street lined with gas lamps. His hand was rough but not hard. He did not pull her along like the man on the farm that morning. Instead, they walked together.

Where are the stars? she thought to herself. Some nights in summer she and the boys would chase fireflies across the yard. The sky had been so dark it was difficult to tell where the fireflies stopped and the stars began. So vast was the sky at home; she knew there was more than this world. Here, with the brilliance of the gas lamps, all but the brightest of the stars were hiding.

She continued two more steps before realizing he had stopped with his arm taut. He drew her closer. His face nearly in hers, Linnea watched his deep brown eyes move back and forth while reading the address pinned to her top. There were flakes of green and gold in his eyes you wouldn't notice from a distance.

He added another new word to her vocabulary, "Woodward." This new word came easier to her in repetition as it was similar to the new word Papa used for chopped timber. He pointed to the building they stood in front of. Stepping closer to the building, he pointed to the numbers which she recognized. This was the address of her destination.

The man in the uniform took her hand again and led her up the four steps to the door. With a solid thumping, his knuckles rapped on the door in short succession. Knock-knock-knock. There was a shift in the weight on the shoulder from the bag, which caused his knees to bend as he shifted his body back under the canvas sack. He looked to Linnea with the slight sadness of a goodbye this time.

"Do you know what hour this is?" The stern voice screeched with the opening of the door.

Her voice and face sent a jolt through Linnea.

"Special delivery," the man in uniform indicated with a head-bob to the side.

Linnea thought the woman's face was made from a series of "V's." The first was the shape of the pointed nose peeking past the door to look onto the stoop. The second was the sharply angled chin which looked like the wedged blade of Papa's ax. Finally, her squinted eyes examined and judged Linnea, each wrinkle of the skin making smaller "V's" bunched together. Her voice creaked, reminding Linnea of the rusted door on the toalett Papa always told Mama he would fix but never did.

As she beckoned, the woman's icy fingers took Linnea by the wrist and pulled her inside. The kind man in the uniform shared another sad last smile as she was yanked past the door that slammed shut.

CHAPTER 2

*L*innea realized the pull on her wrist was a force she couldn't break. Her free hand balled in a fist, ready if needed. The woman she named V continued to talk, leading her down a long dark hallway and up three flights of stairs.

Papa had built a ladder for the boys that went up to the house loft where they slept. She had gone up and down that many times. There were steps in at the Pontiac library. But nothing she had experienced was as high or exhausting as three flights of stairs that seemed to turn and wrap, turn and wrap, turn and wrap, up and up.

On the third floor V took Linnea down another dark hall to an open door. Rows upon rows of beds lined each side of the room, each containing a sleeping person. It carried the functional economy of a military barracks with the grumbling grunts and snores of the pig pen at first feeding. The air was filled with the uneven sound from dozens of raspy inhalations or the wet gurgles of struggling snores.

V had stopped talking. Her gestures grew larger with the wordless mouth movements. She pointed to the empty bed, then at Linnea. The bed, then Linnea. Linnea made the connection. V pointed to the night dress and Linnea at the foot of the bed. Nightdress, Linnea. Linnea slowly took the night dress and put it over her head, keeping a close watch on V. Under the nightdress, Linnea removed her clothes and bent to the floor to pick them up and fold them. Before she could set them on the bedside, V began to gesture again. Impatient, V grabbed the pile from her and shook her head in disbelief. With the lasting icy touch, her long pointer finger signaled again to the bed. Linnea complied and got in under the blanket. It seemed luxurious. She didn't have a mattress at home. There was nothing this soft on the farm. She never had a place for her to sleep alone. Light from the gas lamps on Woodward Avenue caused shadows to dance on the dormitory walls. Her mind played back the children racing to the train and waving from the fields. Horses pulling buckboards and the coach carrying people along the towpath running parallel to the tracks. Before her heavy eyelids closed after the long day, Linnea decided that all of these new experiences would mean she was growing up.

IT WAS STILL DARK when she opened her eyes to the jab in her rib. A bell rang. She recoiled away from the looming figure in the darkness. Linnea's eyes darted, looking for something she knew. This was not home. Where are Mama, Papa, and the boys? It came back to her slowly, the train, the gas lamps, V, and this bed.

The sharp jab in her side was from V, towering over the bed, holding a sneer that mixed pleasure and impatience seeing Linnea jump.

"Hello," Linnea heard a different voice than V. Beside her, an older girl, skin fair like Mama and looking like she could be a cousin, spoke Swedish.

"My name is Elin. This is Miss Stitch. You should call her Miss Stitch. She manages the women's dormitory."

Linnea smiled, "My name is Linnea. It's a pleasure to meet you, Elin. I came in last night from my family's farm."

"We are all from the farm, Linnea. It's nice to meet you," Elin said.

There were a few words between her and Ms. Stitch before the V woman harrumphed and walked away shouting. The bell rang again. Elin looked Linnea up and down, "I am going to help you these first few days. Understand?"

Linnea nodded.

"Here, this is yours. Inside this drawer are your working clothes, a frock. You will get a fresh set every other day. This middle drawer, your unmentionables. This top drawer, put your personal items. This key opens the top drawer. I recommend you lock it. Some people here help themselves to anything and everything. Understand?"

Linnea nodded.

"Put on your clothes."

Linnea got out of bed to comply.

Elin took a red scarf and wrapped it in Linnea's hair, moving the tight pigtails to the back, and folding the scarf over them. "You always wear the scarf, always. Your beautiful blond hair will snag in the machine, and rip your scalp off." Elin turned Linnea to face her in the eye. "Always wear the scarf. Look over my shoulder, three beds past us. The older woman, with the thick eyebrows. Look close, but don't stare."

Linnea did as she was told, and could see there was something different about the side of her face, the skin pink and mangled, her eyebrows painted on, not natural. To see her was spellbinding. The grotesque features, fascinating and inhuman, compelling her to stare. When the woman looked up, she nearly caught Linnea's eyes.

"She screamed in pain for days when it happened. Some of her hair was spared. You could see her skull before the doctor came. Now she's a little dumb. None of the men will look at her or talk to her." Elin repeated, "Always wear your headscarf."

"Always," Linnea said. "Always." *What type of place did Papa send me to?* Linnea thought. "Why are we awake so early?" Linnea asked aloud.

Elin was quick. "Every day we wake up. We will go to the

cafetera. Don't be late, or you won't eat, and you don't want to miss a meal. We work. You are going to be a bobbin carrier."

"Yes, this is an important job."

"This is a hard job. You will work hard, it will not be easy, but every new girl from the farm starts in this position. If you prove yourself capable, you might move to another position. Understand?"

Linnea nodded.

"Come," Eline took her wrist. "We can't miss breakfast."

The two scurried out the door to catch up to the other women of the dormitory. They were already behind. Linnea could sense the urgency of Elin to race ahead, leaving her behind. She did not want to lose her new friend. Linnea hated being left behind.

Linnea's tray was heavy as she carried it to a table. It held beefsteak, eggs, fried potatoes, fruit pie, and hotcakes. Linnea couldn't eat fast enough. Keeping pace with Elin proved difficult.

"You are smart to eat big," Elin said, food in her mouth. "This is it until tonight. Most new girls don't know and go hungry the first day. But I won't let that happen to you."

Linneas tray was still half full when a handbell rang out. Those seated at tables in the far end of the cafeteria stood to form a line with their trays.

"Better hurry, we have minutes at best," Elin said.

Linnea watched as Elin put the beefsteak on the hotcakes and rolled them together. The first of these went into her apron pocket, the second went in her mouth. Linnea imitated her every move, putting the first away, and devouring the second. A third was put into her mouth like a businessman's cigar which she chomped in line while waiting to put her tray away.

A sudden loud roar of machinery caused Linnae to drop her tray. Fear gripped her pumping stomach and she could feel the blood in her face rush away. Elin bent down to the floor to clean the mess. The strong pull on Linnea's apron brought her attention back to the moment. Linnea picked up the tray and thanked Elin.

"That's the line," Elin explained to the white faced girl. "That sound is from the floor you'll be working on."

Linnea could feel the vibration work its way up from the floor to the soles of her shoes and into her arms. *What could these machines be?*

CHAPTER 3

*M*en. There were men in the room in front of an enormous machine. Loud. The machine was loud from rumbling and hissing, and something like the pipe organ from the church warming up and hitting one constant bad note.

A large wheel at one end turned a leather belt and rotated a long rod in the roof. On top of the machine, spinning shafts of twine, being fed by a faster twine. The twine was twisting from a wide band of string feeding into it. The strings came from inside the machine. At the other end of the machine, men shoved rectangular bales of cotton, fluffy, puffy, and soft. The bales arrived through the only door through which Linnea could see. Bale piles stacked high near the train station across the way were as tall as a building.

This station was not the one where she arrived the night before.

Elin had to shout for Linnea to hear, "This is where the men spin cotton on the bobbins before you will get them. But you won't be in here." Elin took her by the wrist breaking the spell the newness cast on her. *Why do people keep nabbing me by the arm?*

The girls journeyed to the opposite end of the large room from the outside loading door. On this far wall steps went up a central corridor. On each side of the steps was a ramp to a framed metal door. Elin led Linnea up the steps to an even larger and longer room.

The women from breakfast now stood in front of a vast number of spinners. A leather band joined to a rotating metal rod from the ceiling connected these machines. The noise, the rumble, and fury of the speed of the spinning shook her to her bones.

"I wouldn't want that job," Linnea shouted. "It looks like one would lose a finger rather quickly." Her words were lost to the rumbles.

No sooner had she finished the words she saw a hand recoil from a near snag. The lady put her finger tip in her mouth to ease the pain of the sting from losing a layer of skin. Index finger in her mouth, she caught Linnea's horrified face from the corner of her eye, and shot her a knowing wink. Linea felt a pang of fright at the sight. It was a cold and knowing look. That lady was tougher than a vagrant or ruffian.

Elin walked Linnea farther down the floor where more machines followed the metal ceiling pole spinning at great speed. A large metal wheel rotated at the end of the line and rod. This wheel, sticking its top third through a hole in the floor, was driven by a chain. Leaning cautiously close, she could see through the floor hole where the rest of the wheel lived. Below, there were more women at machines that looked like tables. Fabrics and felts would join together as each woman took the two parts and made a loud BUZZ through the U-shaped metal bend on the tables. With a turn of the materials, they would send it through the machine for another join, BUZZ. This time the person she was watching did more than nip her finger. The dark squirt shot across the table. She shrieked. The metal needle at the end of the U-shape was penetrating her finger. There was little she could do to move it or her hand away. With her left hand clutching at the table's wheel desperately, she turned it a quarter, moving the needle up enough for her right hand to be free.

Linnea looked to Elin with ghostly shock. She could feel the breakfast try to leave her stomach through its entry path.

To Linnea's dread, instead of calling out for help or leaving the machine, the woman instead reached into her apron pocket to remove a handkerchief. She held firm to slow the bleeding. Next she tied it tight around the injured finger, and bravely continued her task of sewing the joined fabrics.

Elin took Linnea by the hand to continue the tour of the macabre.

She didn't know where they were going, but Linnea didn't want to be here any longer. She wanted to go back to the farm with the chicks and Horse, with Mama and Papa and the boys.

When they got far enough away from the machines for Elin's voice to carry, she said, "Did you see the girl with the cart? She was taking the full bobbins off the machine and placing them in the cart, and replacing it with an empty bobbin."

"The blood from the woman's finger. Her finger! Should we tell someone?"

Elin shook her head. "That happens all the time. Keep working. Did you see the bobbin girl?"

Linnea shook her head.

Elin took her by the hand back into the machine room. She had to tug a second time to overcome Linnea's resistance. "You sure are strong for such a young girl," Elin said, pulling at her, and winning the match of strength.

Elin stopped her in front of hundreds of spools of spinning twine. The woman who had winked at Linnea earlier seemed in a trance now, watching the whirling threads race in the endless circle. The roar of the machine seemed less threatening the longer they stayed. Moment by moment, the machine appeared more predictable. Suddenly there was a POP at the far end. The woman broke from her daydream to quickly pull a pin above the spool that popped. The spin slowed. The empty spool lost speed. When it seemed to nearly stop, the woman tapped its bottom and it shot up and off the pin, sending the spool high into the air. It landed on the far side and danced like a toy top. When it fell, Linnea saw it was a cone shaped piece of wood with a notch on the narrow end.

The woman retrieved a full spool from the bin below her hand. She dropped it on the pin where the empty one had launched from, held the end of the new sting in her hand and quickly laced it through an intricate maze at the top of the machine until the fray was sticking out the top. The thread was pinched in her fingers as she fed the end into the next machine. She next reengaged the release pin to watch this new spool start to spin. In a series of quick successions, the adjacent spool went POP. The next, and another, POP! POP! POP! Now the woman repeated the same task at each spool, unlocking to let them slow their spinning, replacing and rethreading with new spools quickly, locking them back in place to watch them race up again. Each time, the empty wooden bobbin landed from the aerial launch with a distinct strike on the floor. It was an amazing feat to watch. There was a confidence and gracefulness she had never known could happen this fast.

Linnea felt a tug at her arm which she ignored at first. This woman wasn't the ruffian she appeared to be, she was amazing to watch as she repeated this dance time and again flawlessly. The tug returned, stronger. It brought Linnea's attention back to the tour. Elin's words were lost in the noise but her lips moved.

The two walked away from the line to a place where they could hear each other.

"The woman we watched, did you see what she was doing?"

Linnea nodded.

"You are going to make sure she never has to stop. This is important. Do you understand that?"

The little girl nodded again.

"If she stops for more than a minute, the whole factory stops. You need to make sure she always has a full bobbin ready."

Linnea nodded more from habit than understanding. After a moment's thought she asked, "How? I understand this is important, but how can I do this? Show me."

Linnea hadn't noticed the tracks in the floor until Elin pointed them out. They looked like a smaller version of train tracks, similar to the ones that had brought her here. The tracks went to a door behind them and into what looked like a pantry. The two followed the tracks to explore this new room.

Inside were wooden crates filled with twine bobbins. These were the same wooden crates that she had seen at the start of the tour, where the bales of cotton were fed into what looked like Papa's thrasher, with the endless thin twine coming out the other end. Under those wraps of twine must have been the wooden spools. Linnea imagined that these crates, filled with the perfectly placed rolls of twine, had been carried from there to here so they could be given to the woman. In her mind the connections all made sense. Everything worked from one end of the building to the other, in a line.

"But how did they get here?" Linnea asked.

Elin led Linnea out of the room to the opposite side, passing the central door where they entered from the cotton bales for the tour. An identical set of tracks on the floor ran along the far wall parallel to the long line of machines. Here was a closet that mirrored the one they had left. A man with a similar cart to the one filled with bobbins was pushing it out of the room and down the track. This cart was empty. With a nod and a smile he continued his task, pushing a large empty wooden cart forward to where the empty wooden bobbins landed with a crack. The two girls followed him, watching as he picked up the empty bobbins to fill his cart.

Elin tapped him on the shoulder, and pointed to the room where they first saw him. He seemed to understand what she wanted and pushed the cart back into the smaller room. They followed him into the darkness. Linnea was becoming a little scared of what might happen next. A seam of light began to appear at the far edge and grew in size and scale until she realized where there was a door opening. It was like the door on Papa's barn that rolled from right to left. The light filled the little room, showing more spun twine in boxes lining the walls from floor to ceiling.

On the other side of the opened door was the room where the girls had started their tour. Here was the giant machine which ate bales of cotton and spit out the full bobbins. Linnea's bearings were now aligned. This was the door next to the steps and corridor. The room was on the ramp. The door prevented the cart from running away on its own.

They had walked down the line of machines to the far end where she could see through the floor below, and back. This was the line of production for the textiles, to join the fabrics for whatever it was they were making.

The man with the cart pushed until his empty wood bobbins reached the machine. There the empty bobbins were placed on top of pins to collect spun cotton. He walked to the other side of the machine where crates of full bobbins, packed and placed into tight perfect rows, filled another cart, on a similar set of tracks. This cart he pushed back in their direction, up the ramp, to the sliding door, opening to the room of full bobbins.

The elegance of the line, the flow of each task going into the next, each only available when the last task was complete, made the entire tour easy to understand.

"Your job," Elin said, "is the most important. If we can't load the full bobbins fast enough, the whole line stops."

CHAPTER 4

houghts and questions kept Linnea awake in bed long after lights out. Her exhausted body eventually won the struggle with her mind, dragging her into the deepest of sleeps. As she felt her eyes close and mind drift into the fantastic, it was interrupted with the bell and Elin at her side poking her to dress and eat breakfast. She was famished and hot as she stepped into the cafeteria for a full tray and empty table. She knew her responsibility was the *most* important. She ate fast to make sure she was not preventing others from work.

Second out the door, Linnea still chewed as she made her way to the room where a loaded cart from the night before waited. It took her whole weight to move the cart on its track, but the momentum soon kicked in to help. Her entire body was now an anchor dragging behind the cart to slow and stop it in time to align with the machines. As Elin instructed the day prior, she filled the bins below each pin with two extra on top of the bin to complete the task.

With the bins full and cart empty, she paused for a moment and realized how different everything felt when the machines were off. Voices carried from down the line. Outside was a horse neigh that carried through open windows near the roof.

"Linnea?"

She turned to see the woman who winked at her the previous day. "How is your finger?"

"My finger?"

"I saw you get hurt yesterday."

"Oh, that? Nothing. I must do that a few times a day."

Linnea was surprised and stared at her hands.

"Do you want to see?"

"Yes, please."

The woman's hands told a story as she revealed them from her pockets palms up. Radish red at the tips, hard, thick, and callused in the palms.

"They look like my Papa's fingers."

The woman laughed at the remark.

"How old are you?"

The woman smiled. "I turn sixteen in three months. How old are you?"

Linnea chewed her lip and said, "Ten this fall."

"Name is Polly. You're Linnea, right??"

Linnea nodded.

"That's what I thought Elin said."

"She was showing me how everything works."

"You taking her role as bobbin runner?" Polly asked. "Her and me work together good. Do what she tells, you'll be good."

Linnea returned the smile and asked, "How do you move so fast?"

This returned a larger laugh. Polly stepped to the machine and started to explain while working the release pin, the threading maze, and the pinched fray at the top, which she said was hard to do. This was why she'd been on this machine most of the time. She was good with the pinch.

As Linnea watched Polly slowly go through the set-up and explain, Linnea noticed her size. At nearly sixteen she was bigger than her older brother, nearly as tall as Papa. There was a ruggedness about her that Linnea had only seen in boys. When she turned, Linnea noticed she wasn't wearing a frock or dress like other women, but loose pants pulled high. Mama had warned her about women like this, but she had never actually met one before. She didn't know why she should avoid Polly because of pants.

"And that's how I go fast."

A bell rang in another room snapping Polly's attention. She pulled a metal rod on the side which gave a loud CLICK as it released something. The bell stopped, followed by the CHUG of a locomotive. But it wasn't a train. CHUG,

CHUG, CHUG, the sound started to pick up a faster rhythm. Something from above caught her attention. When she looked up, she saw that a rod that ran the length of the roof started turning. As the speed picked up, the bell sounded again. Polly now pushed the lever on the side of her machine forward, increasing the distance between the wheel and rod, tightening the leather strap until it was taut, which caused the bobbins to spin on the machine. The rumble and noise took over her world. There would be no time to talk with Polly and get to know more about her. There was only the task at hand: fill the cart, fill the bins, never let Polly run out of bobbins. It was up to Linnea to keep the factory running.

It was dark outside when the rumbling stopped. Linnea was exhausted after a full day of pushing the cart back and forth on the track. Her chest felt tight with pride. Polly never came close to running out of bobbins. The machines didn't stop once.

Linnea's belly was empty and her sticky skin glowed with perspiration as she made her way to the cafeteria. Before getting in line with the others, she prepped for the next morning, making sure one last time that each bin was full, each box was ready and on the cart.

The supper line seemed longer than the one at breakfast. Her muscles ached as she waited in line to fill her tray. . When she finally got to the food, it was well picked over. She was thankful for the scrapings and broken ends of bread. The water pitcher looked murky and stagnant with floaters and reminded her of the water from the stream at the farm on a hot and lazy day.

Her bed beckoned to her. She dragged her sore feet until she reached her assigned bunk, stripped down, and fell into the mattress. She didn't move again until the morning bell chimed, signaling her to repeat the day.

CHAPTER 5

*A*fter a month in her new vocation, the line had not stopped once. Linnea felt this was important. She felt proud and accomplished in a way she never felt on the farm. It was something she made certain to mention in her first letter home. Ms. Stitch had asked each of the workers to write a letter to be included in that month's pay to be sent back home. Linnea explained how strong she felt now compared to that first week. It was easier to push the cart, at night she was tired but not exhausted, and she had signed up for a class to study numbers.

In her third month, her letter home included the adventure she had on a Sunday when the factory was closed and she could explore the city. Linnea got word a traveling circus was coming to Detroit. It had arrived in America through New York City and was taking the exotic and strange from all over the world through the Erie canal, with stops in Buffalo, Cleveland, and Toledo before arriving in Detroit.

Linnea went down to the riverfront to watch the circus unload from the boat. She wouldn't have the time or money to see a performance. She hoped to catch a glimpse of the wild animals she knew only from stories. As the barge pulled into the dock, the long necks of a pair of giraffes towered out of their crate. The crowd began to grow as the workers unloaded the barge, all hoping to see something fantastic. They were not disappointed as a large, round, bulky creature decided it didn't want to go on land and instead decided to jump into Detroit's river. Its ears wiggled in delight, its eyes above the waterline. The man responsible for the creature cursed at it and gave chase in a smaller boat with his dog. His dog seemed nearly as big as the beast. At first someone next to Linnea thought it might be a trained bear, but the man next to her said it was a large dog called a Mastiff. It wore a permanently sad face with strings of drool continuously dangling from its jowls. The man and the dog filled the little boat. Linnea wondered how they would get the beast on the boat if they caught it.

When the boat got close, the man and dog worked together to coach the animal to the shore. They were so close to Linnea she could hear every swear word the man said, although it was in another language. At times he would get angry at the beast and curse it again, before calming his voice. Linnea's opinion, which she told the couple next to her, was that the Mastiff and beast were friends. The dog was worried about his friend, and that is why the man brought him on the tiny boat. The two politely laughed at the fancy of a small child. That is, until the giant dog jumped into the water and started to swim with the animal, circling it, and leading it to shore. The beast's short fat limbs pushed into the mud, and it waddled up the bank to the man, who was waiting with a rope. The couple agreed the dog and beast must be friends after that. The beast looked like a small elephant without the long nose, and the man next to her called the beast a hippopotamus.

Linnea's letter to the farm after six months included the news that she had completed a third class in math and numbers that would apply to the business of accounting. She wrote to inform them that she had passed a second course in English and writing. Each letter home finished by sending her love to Mama and Papa and her brothers back home. She missed them all dearly.

After that sixth letter home, when the voices of the world were drowned out by the machines and she could only talk to her inner voice, she wondered why there was never a letter returned like she had seen other girls open.

Linnea often had imagined the envelope arriving with money she earned for the family, the letter included, and her handsome brother Abell reading aloud in front of the fire after supper. Abell was a good reader. At the end, Papa would tell Abell to read that one part again. They would laugh at her jokes and smile knowing she did such good work. But she didn't have word from the farm and could only tell herself these things.

As her mind drifted, her heart warm from the thoughts of family and the farm, something happened for the first time. The bell started to ring midday and the machine slowed to a halt. The whir that only happened at dusk happened in the light of the afternoon. Linnea's mind snapped into the clarity of the moment. Her thinking adjusted from the monotonous repetition to understand what was happening and solve the problem. Her eyes grew. Her face dropped, soul began to shrink, and a pain which she had never known before cut at the pit of her stomach. Polly had run out of bobbins.

CHAPTER 6

"*L*innea, do you know what this is?"

She felt small, and answered in a small weak voice, "A map, Mr. Slater?"

"Mr. Slater is my father. Friends call me R.F. Why don't we consider ourselves friends?"

"What does R.F. stand for?" She grew into her chair.

"Rhett Fox Slater is my full name. It is a pleasure to make your acquaintance. "

"It's a pleasure to meet you, R. F."

"I wish it were under better circumstances, Linnea. I understand we had to shut down the line for a full half hour today."

"Yes, sir." Her head hung in shame.

"This map, it's our country, a divided country. Divided because we are in a war. You've gotten word of the war?"

Linnea nodded her head, but only knew the word, not the meaning. There was little she heard from others that didn't sound like gossip. Mama had always told her that gossip was nothing but lies, and she had not raised liars.

"Do you know what we make here, Linnea?"

She shook her head.

"We make uniforms for the Union. Look over here," he turned attention to the map again. "Parts of the uniform are coming from Boston and New York through the Erie Canal, and other parts come from Cleveland and Toledo. By steam train, toe path, boats and barges. Winter is on the way, and our soldiers will need to stay warm. We make winter uniforms with pelts from all over our territory." He looked into Linnea's blue eyes, not sure she had understood. "Do you have brothers?"

"Yes, sir, four older brothers."

"If your brothers went to fight for the cause, you wouldn't want them to be cold, or worse, never get the warm coat they need to fight, would you?"

"Oh, no, Mr. Sla-, I mean, R.F. I would never want that for anyone."

"Miss Stitch tells me you are a good girl who never causes trouble and works hard. I understand you picked up on your duties right off, like duck to water, as they say. I don't want to spend time and money finding someone to replace you and train them. I give everyone a second chance. This is your chance. Would you like to take it?"

"Yes. Yes, I would, R.F. I would like to stay."

"Good. Do not drift again. Stay focused. I do not want to come here after supper like this again."

Linnea could not help but admire Rhett, handsome, assertive, and in control. He also allowed her to call him R.F. because "that's what friends call me." *That must mean,* Linnea allowed herself to think, *we must be friends.* She had never had a friend like R.F. before. Something about this gave her a warm glow inside. No adult had treated her like this before.

"I am sorry you had to cut your supper short to come here."

"Oh, it wasn't trouble. I was meeting with my financier about investments. It was rather dull, I must admit. The textile business is something my father-"

"Mr. Slater?" She quickly added.

R.F. smiled at the interruption, "Yes, my *father, Mr. Slater.* He was the one who started this business. Family is important, he has always said, and when the family is a business, it's important to support the business of the family. I learned the business like you, starting at the bottom and working my way up. I only moved my way up in business after going to school, getting an education, and helping with his business. Education is important and why father, *Mr. Slater,*" he smiled, "makes certain to offer this opportunity to all under his employment."

"Do you have brothers?"

"I have an older brother and a younger sister. You might

say they peaked with me, and it was all downhill from there." R.F. paused for the laughter he always received after the musing, but this time didn't arrive. All that was given was a smile from the pretty girl with blue eyes, blonde hair and interest in what he said. "You see, Linnea, I am a man who suffers from the common symptoms of a normal life. Tireless in work, support of family, thinking of the little man on the street and how they will get by. I suppose I suffer from having too big of a heart for my fellow man."

"You are married and have children?"

"No. I was referring to my fathers, mother, and siblings. More of a family name as a responsibility."

Linnea found R.F. very interesting. He had been to other places and seen things, but they both had a Mama, Papa, and brother. "I wished I had a sister, someone to share secrets with. I only have brothers."

R.F. rose from his chair, his eyes twinkling as he walked around to the front of his desk and sat on its edge, removing the distance between the two. "Sisters are wonderful creatures. My sister's name is Rosmound. She and I would often-"

A rapt door stole the attention. R.F. stood once more and moved to the door, "Yes?"

The metal on the knob turned with the gritty friction as the door opened. "Mr. Slater, a telegram from your father Mr. Slater."

Linnea felt a tickle in her heart hearing this, and thinking *I got to call him R.F. and that man didn't.*

"Thank you, Linnea. I trust you will take our conversation with some thought. You may return to your dormitory."

"Thank you, R.F., sir." Linnea gave a curtsy. As she turned, she saw the man with a telegram at the door, his eyebrows raised at her display.

CHAPTER 7

*E*lin took the seat across from Linnea. She dropped her tray on the table to get Linnea's full attention. "You're still employed, I see."

Linnea continued to chew her food. She believed she had mastered fast eating.

"I understand you had an audience with Mr. Slater."

"R.F. you mean?" she mumbled after swallowing.

Polly sat down next to Elin, her tray also clattering loudly on the table. "Still here?"

"She met with *R.F.* last night."

"Oh, *R.F.*, not even Mr. Slater."

"What did he do? Dock you a month's pay?" Elin shook the table with the aggressive cutting at the meat on her plate. "Dull knives and thick gristle."

Linnea batted her lashes. "Why would he do that?"

"We had to shut the line down, that's why."

"He gave me a warning and another chance. Told me about his sister."

"Oh, I get ya." Polly sounded betrayed. "Told you about his family. Must have made some impression."

"I guess this innocence was all a play, Polly. We really have a tart on our hands."

"Tart? What does that mean?"

"You know," Polly skipped the knife and fork and used her hands, gnawing at the slab, "a woman who is willing."

"I am willing to do good work. Is that being a tart?"

"Depends on the type of work," Polly's laughing brutishness penetrated the little confidence Linnea held onto. Polly chewed her cud, mouth open. "Did you touch it?" Her eyebrows raised. "He ask you to hold it? Squeeze it?"

"It? What do you mean by 'it' Polly?"

Polly winked to Elin, "She doesn't know."

"It's our responsibility to tell her, I guess." Elin winked back

---

LINNEA FELT a release of anger as she pushed the cart with the extra strain of her whole body's weight. She refused to be emotional in front of the other girls. *Mother was right,* Linnea thought to herself as she pushed the full cart. *Gossip is nothing but lies.* She tried to focus her mind on work. She did not want to disappoint R.F. again.

This was the problem, wasn't it? Meeting R.F. was important. He was handsome, a little older, but kind. Not like the gossip and lies from people who were not even in the room during the conversation. *"R.F. is intelligent, not just handsome.* She thought about what his graduation from university would have been like, how he received the framed certificate on his office wall, and how he knew about the war, about trade routes. *He must understand the world.*

As Linnea pushed her cart past Polly, the older girl turned with a devilish look in her eye, and gave a wink. It turned Linnea's stomach to think about what she and Elin described. Linnea took a deep breath as she started to pull back on the cart to slow it. *Focus on the work. Get the bobbins in the bin. Never let the bins get empty. Don't disappoint R.F..*

What they described can't be possible. The size of a looming shuttlecock... He is much taller than me, the size alone! She emptied the bobbins from the cart placing one on top of the other in the bin, balancing the last two on top for added safety. She would not fail again.

Thoughts in her mind returned, haunting Linnea throughout the day. She could not shake the idea planted like a seed in her head by those two and what they said about R.F. No matter how much she worked, how she tried to focus.

She wondered what Abell might say. He would turn work into a game to make the hard times go by faster. She began to challenge herself–how fast could she do a task? How quick could she make the cart go? How swiftly could she load the cart or fill a bin? This worked for a bit, but she realized it only tired her faster. When she was tired, she made mistakes; she dropped a case, failed to stop the cart in time, or cut the timing too close when the next bobbin was needed.

The description Elin and Polly gave played out on the back of her eyelids that night. Weary from the day's work and exhausted from keeping it out of her mind, she succumbed to the thoughts that plagued her throughout the day and allowed herself to imagine. What would R.F. look like if his shirt was unfastened? What would his hands feel like on her, around her in an embrace? What would a kiss feel like from a man without whiskers, clean shaven, and smelling fresh?

CHAPTER 8

$\mathcal{L}$innea didn't say a word. Elin and Polly sat on either side of her, taking turns between chewing and talking. They talked of nothing except boys. The men all worked in one half of the mill, while the girls in the other. The dormitory was clearly separated by floors. Elin and Polly complained that the only man they got to see was old man Higgins, who worked the track opposite of Linnea, taking the empty bobbins to be refilled. The bobbin girl, always the youngest, worked the door nearest the men's side. Each bobbin girl had been too young to appreciate what was on the other side of that door.

Linnea had never thought about it before. She was the bobbin girl, and she did seem to be the youngest. All she wanted was to do her job well, like Mama and Papa taught.

All this talk of boys and men, well, her brothers never said these things.

"I am always ready," Polly said. "Gentel, rough, from behind, or traditional, I am ready. Because once you do it, you own them. You have control over them. They start to do what you say."

"I don't know about that," Elin replied. "The control is more like giving in to the most wonderful craving."

"No, no, it's like taking exercise, or extra work. There is a speed, a rhythm,"

"Like riding a horse?" Linnea interrupted.

The two burst into laughter nearly spilling on the floor.

"Yes, yes, like riding a horse,"Polly said.

"When have you ever ridden a horse?" Elin said.

Linnea noticed two of the women from the line bussing their trays, a sign that Linnea was late. Quickly she shoved more food in her mouth, lifted her tray and scurried to the bus line.

Linnea spent the rest of her day "not thinking" of R.F. or his strong hands, an open shirt, or warm embrace. She wasn't thinking about the possibilities of a chance encounter in the hall, on the street, or being called to his office again. And when she ended the day not thinking about him, she spent her night not dreaming about him. The shadows on the walls didn't take on his profile like the cut paper silhouette made by the man on the corner.

Like many of her Sundays when she had free time because the factory closed, she found herself in the park.

Campus Martius, across from the park, was a public place to see people. Women in dresses with large hats strolled while escorted by their husbands or suitors. Summer was over and the leaves on Michigan's trees dangled for the last of the season in brilliant burnt orange, gold, and yellow. This was her favorite of all the seasons. Everyone on the farm worked into the night, under the harvest moon they stayed in the field almost all night. Autumn might be the loveliest of seasons, but it would lead to the worst: winter. Linnea remembered the stories from what Papa had called the "Hard Winter of '58" when it was cold. Linnea's memory was that Mama's cooking had become different, and "the boys were lean" Mama said.

Linnea longed for her evening classes. She had enjoyed learning and thought she was good at it, but there were no more classes offered that she had not already taken. When she had asked to repeat a course, the instructor said there was not enough interest from other women to host the women's classes. They wouldn't allow her to learn with the men.

When she wrote home, she wanted to tell Mama about the numbers and the writing. There were many new ideas that were part of her thinking, and Mama would be proud of her for learning. When she thought about Mama, with her big arms that jiggled with cotton soft skin and gentle kisses to the forehead at night, her heart warmed. Linnea closed her eyes and imagined Mama's face with kind eyes. The more she thought about her mother, Linnea realized she couldn't remember her voice. This bothered her because it wasn't just her voice she lost, but the words were not coming to her either. Had she forgotten Swedish? *Tonight,* she told herself, *I must talk with Elin in Swedish, not English.*

The beauty of the autumn afternoon with the sun at an angle and large groups of birds singing had been lovely, but it was tinged with longing for her mother as Linnea walked back to the factory. On a corner three blocks from the mill sat a man atop an apple box. He was a beggar man with long, gray, and greasy hair dangling from under his well worn hat. The plaque before him read, "Veteran of Mr. Lincoln's war." As couples passed some would drop a coin in his cup. On closer view Linnea could see that he was blind, missing an eye and the other white with haze. His navy outfit seemed warm, but radiated an unpleasant odor.

"Sir?" Linnea started. "Why does it say Mr. Lincoln's war? Isn't it a war of rebellion?"

His head turned in the direction of her voice, slightly startled that he was being spoken to. "Mr. Lincoln sent me. I hold him responsible." His voice was clear and deep, still strong in timbre. "There is nothing good about war. Mr. Lincoln is not a bad man, but he is still to blame for the dead, the wounded, and the loss of my sight."

"I beg your pardon, sir," a man escorting a woman from the park path said sternly. "I couldn't help but overhear you say to this young lady that the President of the United States was personally to blame for your injuries, and, sir, that is not true. Those southern rebels are at fault. President Lincon provided every opportunity to prevent this escalation."

"You were there, sir?"

"I was not. I certainly appreciate your service, and would not cast judgment against you, sir, for your loss, but it is not true President Lincoln is to blame."

The blind man's head tilted earthbound as if it were heavy to hold up in his grief. "Truth," Linnea could hear the word softly from his lips. The walking cane rolled in his fingers into his tight grip. "Truth," he said with more volume. "When Jesus Christ, our lord and savior, hung between two common thieves on the cross, he said 'I am the *truth*, the way, and the light. No one comes to my father except through me.' But Pontius Pilate extinguished that flame." With a flair of the dramatic, he stood quickly to attention, whipping the cane to the ground and cracking it on the walk. "Heroditus was known as the father of *lies* in his time, but throughout the centuries of humanity's maturation, trained minds found *truth* in his writings following his passing. This is 'The Example of Truth;' because where there are *lies*, there must be *truth*. There cannot be one without the other. And, good sir, no matter how well your intentions, the truth escapes you. Mr. Lincoln will go down in the ages as the cruelest, unable to see what a blind man can. War is the weakness that will bring down all mankind. It is the greatest sin of all to kill, and he sends men to commit this act each day."

The face of the passerby was frozen, stunned and confused by the passion and clarity of an argument that had no retort. With a tug at the arm by the lady at his side, she said, "Let us go now, Roger."

As they left, the pace of the street returned to normal, and the blind man sat back down on his box. With his cane firmly in hand, he said in a more amiable tone, "Thank you, young miss, for talking to me. It has been a lonely and long time since I've had the pleasure of someone's company. I hope that my words didn't scare you."

"A little." Linnea admitted. "I work at the textile mill. We make the uniforms for the North. Everything is loud there, the volume didn't shake me."

"My uniform kept me warm through my first campaign. Thank you for doing such a good job."

"Do you believe that? What you said? That there must be truth because there are lies?"

"I do," he nodded. "Truth tellers are damned. We tell lies to avoid damnation."

"I thought lying was a sin."

"Treachery, yes."

"Sinners are damned as well?"

"We all are, young miss. We all are."

CHAPTER 9

The stone steps to the mill was Linnea's second favorite place to sit and watch people. She could see to the corner of Woodward where the rush, the push, and the flow were heavy, even on a Sunday afternoon.

The words of the blind man lingered in her mind, "where there are lies, there must be truth." She was both confused and intrigued by the idea. She knew of church. She knew of the President, and Jesus Christ. But the other words and names lost meaning to her. Mama told her about sin. She also explained that we are good people who don't sin, and should avoid it. Linnea had never questioned if there was a truth, or if anything was true. The birds were birds, they sang a song, made nests, and flew. There must be truth in nature. Nature does not lie. People could lie, she decided, because they were above nature. People have souls, and this is what allows them to lie, to sin. It was a choice.

Linnea found a small rock, and wrote out the phrase on the steps, "where there are lies, there must be truth." She thought the sentence looked like an equation in math, lies and truth were opposite sides.

The blind man's logic seemed to say that if there was a lie, there must be truth. Lies and truth were equations, and they must balance. This is what she had learned in class. The properties of equality. On both sides of the equal sign the value must balance. If truth was on one side, lies would be on the other. They could not be alone, Truth needed other values to balance the value of lies, because it could not calculate on its own that Truth = Lies, or Lies = Truth. What were those other values to balance the equation?

"Linnea? What are you doing here?"

Linnea was startled from her thoughts. "R.F.!"

He smiled. "Shouldn't you be with friends? Or having your supper? Why are you sitting on the stoop all alone?"

"Supper isn't served on Sundays in the dorm. Only breakfast and late lunch. They give the kitchen the evening off."

"No companions?"

She shook her head, "What about you R.F.? Why aren't you with friends or at supper?"

"Well, I thought about supper and started to walk to get some, but thought about some papers on my desk, and found myself here instead, with you."

"What is the paper on your desk?"

"It's a letter from my father. He tells me that the British textile workers have stopped working."

"I thought that the line couldn't stop."

"Well, for us, that's true. But these British workers refuse to work from cotton picked by the south. They oppose slavery like we do in the North."

Linnea didn't fully understand everything R.F. had said, but he was more learned. He had the certificates on the wall as proof.

"When the British workers refuse to take cotton from the South, that means these goods become what is called scarce. Scarcity of a thing raises the price people are willing to pay."

"Do we get our cotton from the South?"

"My father purchased great stores of cotton prior to the war, we've been producing with that stock this year."

"Do you think our line could stop? Would the workers here refuse to work with cotton from the South?"

R.F. thought for a moment, "I certainly hope not. You pose an interesting question. You are very clever for asking that. I find you to be a rare commodity, Linnea."

Linnea could feel the warmth in her cheeks glow and a flutter in her heart at hearing his praise.

"Would you care to continue this conversation in my office? I can read you the letter directly."

CHAPTER 10

"*L*ate to bed last night," Elin noted. "I thought you might have been taken by savages."

"That's no joke," Polly barked. "I have people taken by savages."

"I didn't know," Elin said.

Linnea didn't say a word. She focused on eating quickly and watching the door for the line to form.

Sincerity crept into Elin's voice. "I was only worried about our friend Linnea. It's not like her to be out late."

"I say she has a secret place."

"Like a hiding spot?"

"A place only she knows, where she can be away from others."

"What do you say, Linnea?" Elin asked.

Linnea smiled as best she could muster while chewing

until she was able to say, "That would be nice." With one more shovel of food into her mouth, she stood, taking her tray to the return. The walk to the tray drop seemed farther away this morning. The other girls were right. She had been up late and was tired.

She felt sore as she filled the cart. Too much walking in the park, down to the river, to the station, over to stables to see horses, back to the park, and to the steps. But there was something magical about spending time with R.F. and learning about the rest of the world. She felt such confidence and trust in him for his keen head. Something in her felt strange looking in his eyes, and she enjoyed listening to him talk for long stretches of time. The topic didn't matter. Being with him created such energy, excitement, that she wasn't sure she could contain it at times. Linnea thought she did a good job acting like a normal person might. Maybe she had eaten too fast. She felt bloated and achy. And feeling sore may not have been entirely from walking.

"ARE you going to show us your special place?" Polly asked as the sounds of the machine lowered.

Linnea had filled all the bins and was now in her storage room, filling the cart for the next morning and clearing the shelves where fresh bobbin crates could stack. "What makes you think I have a secret place?"

Polly shrugged, watching from the entrance. "You seem the type."

"There's a type?"

"Always, for everything."

As she staked the last few bobbins on top of the cart, Linnea wondered out loud, "What other types are there?"

"There is the type like you and me, who work hard. There is the type like those big-hat ladies on Sunday in the park. They don't hardly do a thing but look pretty."

"All done," Linnea declared. "Let's go."

Linnea and Elin slowly walked back to the dorm. There was non-stop talk about the types of people in the world. A type who was honest to a fault, a type who lied. Ones who you could trust, others that were snakes in waiting. Types that were intelligent but condescending, those who were simple and looked up to you to help. There were all kinds of types of people in the world, as Polly described it, were either like her or the opposite.

The two parted ways when Linnea wanted to clean up. Polly didn't care how she smelled to others. She went directly to the dormitory. A wet towel in Linnea's hand did wonders to wipe away the evidence of the day's work. There was a freshness that returned Linnea's state of mind to clarity. In her private cleaning she discovered blood. It made her think hard about what it could be and filled her head with worry. There wasn't much blood, but why should there be any? Linnea remembered how she felt that morning, bloated and sore in places that normally weren't. That feeling of eating too much, drinking too much.

After she dressed, she found Ms. Stitch alone for a private moment. In hushed tones, away from the others, Ms. Stitch tried to explain and find the right words. The little V's that made up her mouth sharpened in angle and shape to form a smile. Ms. Stitch excused herself and returned with some wadded fabric in her hand, and whispered instructions in Linnea's ear.

The wad seemed to be some sort of underwear designed with thick cotton in a specific region. Linnea put them on to realize the discomfort immediately, but with a little wear and a few steps, things seemed to measure up and feel nearly normal.

In the morning Linnea was the first to the table. She was already eating when her two companions joined her. Linnea greeted them in Swedish, and tried to engage Elin to practice. Elin, who had been speaking English longer than Linnea, was having difficulty.

"I know the sentiment, but the words are difficult," Elin admitted.

"This is why I thought we should practice."

"To what end? Are you going to Sweden?"

"No, but I want to go home one day and see Mama and Papa again."

"That would be nice," Elin's bottom lip drooped, she inhaled quickly to prevent the tears which came easily when discussing family. "I've thought about going home many times. But I am never sure they would want to see me again. They did send me here."

"But they get part of your wages. They needed you to contribute, didn't they?"

When Elin didn't answer, Linnea asked again. "Why do you look at me like that? Didn't they?"

"Linnea, we don't know that's true. Maybe Mr. Slater and the mill send them money, but maybe they don't. I've never gotten word back. Have you?"

Linnea looked at Polly. "No. Never a letter. Not one. Don't know who could write one back. I've lost my appetite." Linnea lifted the tray from the table and returned it, slowly marching off to her labor, uncertain of the reasons she was there, or if there was anything more to this life but keeping R.F.'s line running.

CHAPTER 11

*I*cy crystals formed at the edges where the glass met the pane's edge on the dormitory windows. Moonglow reflected off the cold lines making the world seem beautiful. Linnea had counted the thirty-four days since last seeing R.F. before his trip back east on the steam train. She thought of him every night. Part of her wanted to climb out of this bunk, find a horse, and ride through the night to Massachusetts with the speed of Paul Revere, calling out to find him. She wanted him to hold her again. He would tell her amazing things she had never imagined. The other part of her wanted to sleep. Her body was worn out, and she knew that in the morning she would do the same thing she had done nearly every day since arriving: keep the line moving.

Linnea stirred before the bell with stomach troubles. At

first she thought it might be something she ate, or didn't eat. As her world became more clear, she counted the number of weeks since she wore those absorbent panties Ms. Stitch provided. Ms. Stitch had told her she would need them about every four weeks, but it had been roughly six weeks. And this seemed different. A loud gurgle from her belly croaked, and she was in urgent need of the chamber pot. The speed at which this sickness came did not allow her to make it to the privy. Her retch was clear and left a foul taste in her mouth, and it came up again. Twenty minutes had passed before she was able to leave the privy.

She was truly miserable, her heart aching over R.F. and her body in pain curled on the floor with the pot. She gave in to the sweet release of sleep on the uncomfortable floor, her eyes finding comfort in the dark.

"Miss Stitch!" a voice shouted over Linnea, waking her. "Miss Stitch, Linnea is ill."

Her eyes opened. Heart pumping, she tried to get to her feet, nicking the pot on her way up. At full stance, Linnea met the eyes of Ms. Stitch, the V's of her squinted eyes sharing disappointment in each wrinkle. Linnea could feel the ooze of cold sick from the spilled pot on her foot and ankle.

"Ill? Are you ill? How are you ill?"

She wasn't sure how to respond. Instead of answering Linnea stood there in misery.

"Well?" Ms. Stitch said. "Clementine, clean up this mess,

use hot water and vinegar. You," she pointed to Linnea, "follow me. You are going into isolation."

Stepping forward, Ms.Stitch looked back, "Come, come, now. Don't dilly dally."

Linnea followed instructions and began to walk forward. As she passed full beds, some pulled their blankets to their faces in shock and disgust. Those standing gave way, stepping back several feet to make a path.

The two arrived at a private room with a lock. It had a bed, a window, and a large brass tub. At the edges of the waterline those same frosty dendrites of the icy window from the night before, which magically caught the moon's reflection, held true to the water's surface.

"Don't you worry. We will get you some hot water for a bath. Rest here, and do not open the door for anyone," Ms. Stitch said.

The door closed followed by a click of the latch to keep her inside. Linnea pulled on the tight bedding tucked under the mattress and got beneath the covers. Being ill here, alone, was a new experience. Linnea hated being alone. She wanted to see Mama and Papa. Somehow this wouldn't be as awful if Mama were here.

The distant roar of the machine starting and the rattle of the window told her the line had started the day without her.

"I've let them down," she cried to herself. "I've let down R.F., too."

CHAPTER 12

"I hope to never be locked away from everyone again."

"I am sorry to hear that you went through this ordeal," R.F. said. "You see, we can not afford to have illness spread to others. Imagine if you had Scarlet Fever, or worse Typhoid. If you were to expose others, and they were unable to do work, the whole line would stop. We would not have enough people." He twisted his hands together in uncertainty. "You said earlier that you felt you had let me down and that is not true. You may have saved my business by being in isolation for these last weeks until my return... if you were truly ill."

"Yes, if I were ill," she said, looking down. "Thank you."

"Would you care for some water?" He adjusted his tie that felt tighter than normal. He pointed to the pitcher. "This was brought fresh from the pump house."

"Yes, please. Thank you."

R.F. rose from his desk to lift the pitcher and pour into the glass. It was clear and made the etched design reflect the light. Their fingers touched as he handed it to her. This brought her a sense of delight feeling his touch again, even if just for an instant. He nearly dropped the glass at the surprise sensation.

"We've known each other for a few months now. It seems odd for this conversation to be difficult as it is."

"Is it difficult?" she asked.

"Well, yes, in part. Our positions in life are different, you and I."

"Are they?"

"Yes. I mean, my life's experience includes ocean voyages, steam trains, formal education, and a work ethic of commitment to the family honor. And it is not to say you do not have or share that honor or a type of commitment. More, I mean to say, there is a public image one must uphold to keep that honor." He stopped. His words had not been received with the depth intended.

Outside the door of his office one could hear others performing their daily tasks. R.F. adjusted his sitting, took a more casual position on the edge of his desk, crossed his arms, and spoke in a lower tone others would not overhear. "We're different, you and I."

"I did take a train here. We've both been on a train."

"Yes, that's true."

"And I find your stories to be brilliant. You understand

business, and the world, and numbers. You do know much more than me. That's what I enjoy about our relationship."

R.F. nodded, "We are friends, are we not?"

"For all we've done and said, I hope," Linnea searched for the right thing to say, "more than friends. You tell me you suffer the common symptoms of a normal life, but you are much more than normal to me, R.F., and I want you to know that."

"Yes, that is sweet, and I would like for nothing more for that to be true in exchange. Linnea, you are a scarce treasure in this world and have great value."

"All I want is a chance to be with you. You could still do everything you want, let me be by your side."

"Linnea. I adore you, but I have obligations. Which is why you and I can never be together, again, no, not like that." The words were a quick sting. "You were telling me that you did not enjoy this isolation, you wanted to be with other people, outside of that room. I care enough about you, Linnea, enough that I want to propose a clever plan that will be best for both of us. Are you interested to hear the plan."

Her face lit up with hope. He had made a plan. That meant R.F. had been thinking about her in great detail. She was part of his plan, his life.

"My financial advisor has friends, dear friends. They are unable to have children after trying many times."

"That's awful."

"Yes, tragic. They are good Christians who want nothing more than to have a child to love and care for, but they are unable to create a family of their own. They would be interested for you to stay with them over the next several months. You will live in their house. They will care for you, look after you, and when things come to a certain time, they will take responsibility. Do you understand?"

Linnea's shoulders dropped as she slouched into the chair and slowly nodded acceptance while he explained. Linnea felt smaller with every word in a world that was rapidly growing, putting distance between them. She noticed the skin on her hands looked dry, and started to pick at the white blotches that started to spread from the weeks in isolation. Linnea started to pay more attention when he said, "I can tell you do not like this idea. This is actually a good plan."

"It's a good plan. It's just... I had hoped the plan involved more time when you and I were together."

"Yes, that would be nice. I would enjoy that, but it would not be fair to you, and it would be irresponsible to the duty I have to my family."

"I understand," Linnea said. She felt like curling up and crying.

"There are parts of this plan I have yet to explain."

"There is more?" Hope rose within her chest, her chin shot up.

"During this time, I will continue to send your pay to your family. At the right time, this couple will also provide you with a settlement."

"A settlement? Like land?" Her head tilted.

"Not quite. This settlement will be in cash. The sum will be substantial, and if properly looked after, my advisor tells me it should last you several years."

"And my new job would be to stay with this couple?"

"That's right. They will look after your every need."

"And you?"

"I will stay here and make sure that we keep the line moving, that it never stops," he said. "You want that, correct? You said you would feel bad if it were to stop on your behalf, and, well, I don't know that you can keep the line running for the next few months as things progress."

She looked to the floor unable to meet his eyes. Linnea found the truth, like in many cases, to both follow logic and to be cruel. She realized she was the problem to be solved, and there was no way to balance this equation without leaving. She could feel that ache in her heart again. She wasn't sure it would ever stop.

A short rap at the door took her attention. The voice on the other side was familiar. Ms. Stitch said simply, "They're here."

CHAPTER 13

*L*innea's second train ride was with passengers, not mail service. The excitement of the trip wore off by the time she left the boundaries of Detroit. Looking out the window allowed her mind to drift and reflect. Linnea thought back on the time she had spent in isolation. The weeks she had been forced to stay in that room without real interaction gave her deep grief and anguish. Her examination by the doctor, a complete stranger, was the only human contact she had received until she saw R.F. She could hear when others came to the door, sliding meals through the bottom slot. Quick to leave, none engaged in conversation no matter what Linnea said, asked, or pleaded. Elin and Polly, who she had considered friends, or at least friendly enough, did not come to visit. One late night she was sure that the heavy mouth breathing of Polly waited outside the door, followed by her brutish footsteps stomping away. Still no word, not a single kindness.

These were the things she was leaving behind: difficult work that could maim and mangle; people who cared little for others, spread gossip, and told filthy stories of indecent acts; and the ugly imprisonment and isolation imposed by "Ms. V". Still, she would also lose the one person who cared for her, treated her kindly, became a true friend, and explored a part of her she never knew existed, something powerful to feel. To protect herself and to protect his family, she would find this new part of life.

Desperate to be with others, Linnea tried to speak with other passengers. The man next to her was only interested in his paper and would not engage. The woman across from her resisted making eye contact. Linnea didn't know what to call the expression. The results were always the same: disinterest in her. It was as if Linnea was out of place being in the train car. Maybe she would do better with the bags of posted mail. She didn't feel worth the Penny Black stamp that had gotten her this far.

She was nervous as the train rolled into the Jackson train station. The single story red brick building was almost as long as the train from engine to caboose. People were everywhere, some ready to meet travelers or unload cargo, others waiting to occupy an empty seat for other destinations like Chicago, Lansing, or Saginaw.

Waiting on the platform, Linnea wondered what this couple looked like. She had no bags, no personal items only her headscarf and the used wax wrapper from the sandwich given to her in Detroit by R.F. 's rather large business associate who had escorted her to her seat on the train. The wax wrapper could be of use again.

Once the excitement of the train's arrival began to wane, the conductor called, "All aboard!" for the departure. The klaxon rang out its warning, and the initial CHUG-CHUG of the engines' main wheels started the forward momentum on the track. Moments later she waved to the man standing on the back deck of the caboose. The thought occurred to Linnea at that moment that there might not be a couple waiting. *What if R.F. wasn't telling the truth? How long should I wait here? What could I do next? I hate being alone.* She knew these thoughts were influenced by the voices of Elin and Polly and their doubts that the money was sent home at the end of each month.

Linnea could feel the press of wood against her bones during the second hour of sitting on the bench. She was on the only bench at the station still in the sun, trying to keep warm. In another quarter hour or so, the sun would set. Her next option would be to go inside the station, but it wasn't much warmer there. Still, she felt the platform was where most others would naturally meet for arrivals.

In the distance another train bell rang out. On approach, the whistle blew and the steam shot across the platform, giving her a blast of warmth she wished would last while she watched a new group of passengers board. Only a few departed the train here. With a call out, "All aboard," Linnea welcomed that CHUG-CHUG forward, wishing those travelers safety.

As cars rolled by, pulled by the engine, she noticed the open door of the mail car. Hanging his head out was the same young man in uniform who had taken her to Detroit. His eyes connected with hers and that moment of recognition between the two was immediate. There was nothing they could say over the bell and roar. He gave a limp wave in time for her to return the gesture, a moment of two people connecting in a shared memory from almost a year ago in this great big world. Linnea wished she knew his name. She should have asked for his name. They had spent a day together. When she was locked away, she had thought about that day many times.

"Linnea?" a woman's voice called out.

She turned to see a handsome couple approach. The man dressed like R.F., and the lady wore a big hat like one of those women in the park on Sundays.

"Linnea? How long have you been waiting here?" the woman asked.

"Since the afternoon train."

"That was nearly three and a half hours ago!" The man raised his eyebrows in surprise. He pulled the pocket watch from his vest. "Damn this thing must still be broken."

"That sounds right, three hours."

"Oh, dear child, we had got word you would be on the evening train from Detroit, the one that just left the station. I am sorry to have kept you waiting. How do you feel? Are you well? Do you feel ill?"

"I am fine, thank you."

"Where are our manners?" The pocket watch open in his left hand snapped shut with a click, and in a well practiced movement he tucked it into his vest pocket, "Linnea, I am Benjamin Baxter and this is my lovely wife, Ellen." The dangling watch chain swayed with his arms movement dazzling in the remaining light.

"Ellen Beaumont is my maiden name."

Linnea wondered if they expected her to know those last names by the way they said them. Or maybe this is what posh people did. This might be how the ladies with big hats in the park spoke to one another. She smiled, and gave what she thought was a curtsy, "Mr. Baxter, Mrs. Baxter."

The couple looked at each other, unsure of the gesture.

"Well, Linnea, it is a pleasure to meet you," Mr. Baxter said. "We have a warm coach waiting to take us to Hillsdale. The train between Jackson and Hillsdale only runs once a day now with many of the boys heading to the fight. Now, if you wanted to go south, you would have a dozen options."

"Do you have anything we should take to the coach?" Mrs. Baxter asked. "A trunk, maybe? Or luggage?"

Linnea shook her head. "I don't have any of those things."

"A change of clothes? A jacket?" he asked.

"No. It's me and this wax wrapper." She held it up for show.

"Oh, Benjamin," Mrs. Baxter said, tugging on her

husband's arm, "we should feed this poor girl before we travel."

"Yes, agreed."

Mr. Baxter went to speak with the coachman while Mrs. Baxter took Linnea to the Cooper Street Dining Saloon. Mr. Baxter rejoined the ladies inside where they enjoyed a table near the fireplace.

"I don't think we've been here since the summer of '54" Mr.Baxter said.

"That was a warm July, and so many people!" Mrs Baxter smiled at the memory. "I recall being happy to be seated."

"That was a good day, a good cause. A grand old party. It got Lincoln to Blomington."

"Blomington got Lincoln to the White House."

Mr. Baxter ordered three chicken dinners for the table. When the food arrived, Linnea started to eat at the speed she was accustomed to from life in the factory. Everything went in too fast to chew.

"Dear girl," Mrs. Baxter said, scandalized. "Please slow down before you hurt yourself."

"What?" Linnea asked with a full mouth.

"Linnea," Mrs. Baxter snapped. She composed herself and sternly said, "Mr. Baxter and I are people of principles. We don't want to impose them on you, but we would ask out of courtesy–"

"And health," Mr Baxter interrupted.

"And health," she parrotted, " that you eat slower and

chew your food completely. This is a meal, not a foot race. The coach will wait for us."

"I suspect that they did not teach manners at the textile mill. Is that correct?"

"Numbers. I learned numbers and writing."

"Yes, both are excellent ventures to expand the mind. We have many great minds on each of these topics at the college."

"College?"

"Yes, Mr. Baxter is a professor at Hillsdale College." Mrs. Baxter beamed with pride for her husband.

Linnea nodded and returned her attention to her plate. Instead of picking up more chicken with her fingers, she opted to use the fork next to her plate this time, a habit her Mama had insisted on when she was at home but she had ignored since she worked at the factory. She smiled at the Baxters. Both smiled in return. Linnea fought the urge to eat fast. She had time now. She didn't have to run to the line and stack bobbins. Chewing her food, tasting the chicken, she realized that it tasted good. It wasn't simply cooked. There was salt and spices on the chicken. The potato was mashed, not boiled and cut in half. There was butter to savor. The corn was yellow, not white and brown, and it actually tasted like corn. The whole meal was a reminder of her time on the farm when there was food to eat.

"Which do you prefer?" asked Mr. Baxter. "Working with numbers or writing?"

"Numbers," Linnea replied. "I was better at numbers, they

made more sense and had fewer rules. With writing, you have to know the rules for spelling a word, the order for the word next to others, and which makes more sense in what order. Not to start on punctuation. So many rules and too many exceptions to them."

"Numbers have more logic to them?"

"Yes. The power of the equal sign makes more sense somehow. There is always balance. The rules have a predictable outcome."

"Did they teach you about algebra?"

"What's that?"

"A higher level, more advanced math, numbers."

"Tell me more about this math. Numbers I like. Algebra? Math? There is more to numbers?"

"Much more."

DURING THE COACH ride Linnea slept nearly the entire trip. It was dark when they arrived at the home of the Baxters. Lights in the windows of the two-story house lit the yard and looked magical. Walking up the steps, she could see the porch was wide and ideal for sitting to watch passersby on the street. Rich, deep wood floors and walls that were hung with paper were a first for Linnea. The stairs inside the home welcomed her to go up. It was sandwiched on the main floor with a sitting room on the left rail side, and dining room on the right rail side.

"This is nothing like the farm," she said.

"You are a welcomed guest here" Mrs. Baxter started up the stairs. When Linnea didn't follow, she added, "Let me show you to your room."

"My room?"

"Yes, you will have your own room here, on the second floor."

Once under the covers of her bed, snuggled away from the evening chill, Linnea said aloud to no one, "And I thought the bunk at the textile mill was comfortable."

CHAPTER 14

*B*risk walks each morning came at the insistence of Mrs. Baxter. She would rise before the sun and make certain Linnea had a warm outfit in which to make the morning constitutional. Mrs. Baxter suggested, on more than one occasion, that the hymn from Sunday's service, "What a friend we have in Jesus," was the ideal rhythm for pace.

This new experience of regularly attending church provided Mrs. Baxter every opportunity to lend a fancy dress and hat. Linnea felt uncomfortable after the hour it took to dress. She sat as best she could, feeling the hard wood of the pew on her tailbone. There were times squirming was irresistible from the flashes of heat or chill through her body. When the day came that none of the dresses, even let out, would fit, she was no longer required to attend service.

Introductions to neighbors and members of the congregation were under the veil of what Mrs. Baxter called a white lie. She explained that Linnea was her niece staying with them for the season. The expanding dress sizes on Sunday, or layers of additional winter coats during walks, could not hide the growing truth peaking out to spoil the lie.

"Gossips," Mrs. Baxter complained. "Now eat your breakfast. *Slowly.*"

Mr. Baxter flipped his newspaper down to add, "What's important is your health, Linnea. It's better to stay inside for now. I worry those icy paths will do you harm."

Her stay was different from the isolation she had experienced at the factory. Here, she wasn't alone. However, the only three people in her life included the Baxters and their cook. The Baxters provided continued guidance, instruction, and oversight. The cook hardly said a word. Instead a little bell from the kitchen would tinkle when meals were ready to be served.

The reflection from the full length mirror in her bedroom captured her disappointment. Her body seemed unrecognizable from what it used to be. When she was working the line, her body had been tight and youthful, strong and agile. Today, she was plump and bulky, slow and lethargic. She was most certainly her mother's daughter.

Within a few weeks' time, Linnea could hardly stand in front of the mirror, let alone stand what she saw. The stairs seemed insurmountable. Going down each step was a cautionary endeavor, working to prevent a fall. Each step up an expedition placing the handrails bearing in question. Rather than traverse the stairs, she lay in bed. On that first night she had believed the mattress was a heavenly bliss. Now, it was a medieval torture device where she could find no level of comfort. A few moments on her back, and she couldn't breath. Rolling to one side found a new level of stress. Rolling to the other side she discovered strain. Any attempt to sleep on her stomach was laughable.

A new pain came without warning. The intensity forced her to call out in the night. Mrs. Baxter arrived at the door by lamplight.

"Stand her up. Help her walk," Mr. Baxter instructed. "Put the pot on the stove, boil the water, and gather clean sheets. Quickly now!"

Reflections of light from the lantern traced the glow from Linnea's brow. Mrs. Baxter helped her up by the arm. She used her free hand to wipe away the droplets of perspiration near her eye in dramatic swipes.

"We have to help this go quickly," Mr. Baxter repeated. "Time is essential."

Softly, Mrs. Baxter sang her hymnal trying to keep rhythm in her step. Linnea could hardly advance each limb under the duress, until finally her knees buckled as she made a noise like a hurt animal.

The cook had tended to the hot water and clean bedding while Mrs. Baxter had walked with Linnea. When the bed was ready, both Baxters and the cook had to work together to get Linnea back into bed. Nearly scalding hot towels cleansed Linneas body. Despite the care and tenderness with which she was washed, Linneas skin became highly sensitive and irritated.

The cook stepped out of the room for a moment and returned bringing a trail of fresh, cold winter air with her and said, "Here, dear, chew on this." Linnea was presented with one of the large icicles she had watched growing off the porch roof as she peered out of the sitting room window. Its thick end was wrapped in another towel for her to hold. In her mouth, it felt cold, perfectly distracting from everything else. Each crunch between her teeth was delight in the moment, the first relief she had felt in some time.

A new wave started through her body, this time a tsunami, as she pushed and worked harder than any day on the line. This felt like ten times the weight of the bobbin cart on her first day. Her body turned rubber after. A gasp came from Mrs. Baxter, followed by the cry of new life.

CHAPTER 15

"My little man," Mr. Baxter said.

"Look at how beautiful he is," the cook said. "All babies are beautiful, but this one… my, oh, my."

"My dear, why are you crying?"

"He… he's perfect," Mrs. Baxter said.

Linnea felt like an empty vessel. All of the attention had turned away from her to the baby. Burned out from the ordeal, her last memory was the blue light of the winter dawn illuminating the second floor window of that room. The cook cleaned the mess with scalding hot towels. Linnea didn't care.

Swaddled in a pink birth cloth that Mrs. Baxter had inherited, the baby was handed to Linnea. Nature took over, the baby latched on and fed until satisfied. Both mother and child fell asleep.

LINNEA WASN'T TRYING to listen in on the private conversation. In the still of the night it was difficult to avoid what was said as the voices carried through the walls and floor. While the baby slept by her side she could hear the two talk.

"What can we do?" Mr. Baxter said. "We can't keep them both."

"We could tell the baby that Linnea is his older sister. We can raise them as siblings."

"And the good people of Hillsdale? There is only one miracle birth I am aware of."

"Every birth is a miracle. You saw how things progressed." Mrs. Baxter used the sweet tone she reserved for when she wanted her way. "They are our niece and nephew. We just don't say anything. Why do we need to tell our neighbors anything?"

"There will be talk. And there is the code of conduct I have agreed to follow. You and I are good, honest people. We can't lie. Not about this. Not like this. It will take us down a path we don't want to travel."

"We could find a new college or university where you could teach. Hillsdale is ideal, but there must be similar opportunities we could find. Maybe out west? Or the city?"

Linnea liked the idea of staying. Linnea hated the idea of being alone. She had grown fond of the Baxters. They treated her like family, but the type of family who didn't send their child to the textile factory. The kind who were quicker to provide a hug, a touch, or a tender moment. She didn't recall this with Mama. Mama was always a little distant and sparse with affection. On a night like this Papa would tell a story and kiss her good night. The Baxters were affectionate and caring in ways Linnea wasn't familiar with, causing her to wonder which family was more normal. *Had I been missing out on something on the farm?*

THE NEXT THREE weeks were repetitive. Linnea noticed the predictable pattern that she automatically produced milk at the sound of his cries. No name for the child had been chosen yet. A list of family names continued in a similar pattern, and every time the topic came to discussion, Linnea found herself ignoring what was said, lost in a world that was populated by only the baby and her.

Baby was slow to take to the glass banjo-shaped bottle with rubber nipple Mr. Baxter had bought during his recent trip to Jackson. There were three such items in the collection which held the goats milk from the yard. The cook said they were easy to warm and clean.

Mrs. Baxter was insistent on caring for the baby once he started taking the bottle. Linnea watched from a distance as Mrs. Baxter took care of diaper changes, putting the baby to bed, play time, baths, and being rocked to sleep in her arms.

Linnea felt like she had that first night, an empty vessel, finished with her purpose.

Alone, under the cover of a thick throw, Linnea's limbs dangled from the porch swing on the first day warm enough to melt snow. She thought about R.F.'s plan as the lazy momentum kept her in a back and forth motion. The Baxters were decent people. She wondered how they might take good care of her and of Baby. She loved Baby. She wanted to keep and care for him herself but knew that she was in no position to do so. This was not the plan.

Linnea thought to write to R.F. to inform him his plan was a success. *He would be interested in Baby, wouldn't he?* She thought that those who could write to her and had cared, would have done so. But there had been no word from R.F. since she left. Linnea may not be a consideration to him. After all, he had a duty to his family, to the company, to the line. If R.F. were true to his word, payments would be made to Mama and Papa. There was no reason to believe he wasn't a man of his word.

Linnea thought back to her numbers. She tried to formulate an equation of what to do next. If she wrote to R.F. about Baby, he could stop sending payment to Mama and Papa. That was the plan he described. There was also the plan of the settlement. According to R.F.'s plan, the baby would be a Baxter, and Linnea would have the settlement. *What if I could also be a Baxter?*

After taking a winter coat, Linnea began to walk the path for her morning constitutional. Through the streets of Hillsdale she passed by the large houses, her feet taking her into town. She looked in the windows of the shops until she reached the college. Her single lap around the campus turned her back, passing the shops again and toward the house.

This time through town she noticed a different type of look. She thought of the people on her second train who had ignored her. Now, people could not take their eyes off her.

Two boys half her age started to keep pace with her.

"Are you with the Baxters?" one of the boys asked.

"I am."

"Are you really Mrs. Baxter's niece?"

"I am with the Baxters."

"My mother says you're a fallen woman. What did you fall from?"

"I'm sure I don't know."

"My father," the other boy said, "says you carried a bastard."

"Yeah, my father said that too. Said you were a bitch."

"Lady, do you know what a bastard is?"

"Or a bitch? What is that?"

Linnea stopped walking and looked to the two inquisitive boys. She wasn't sure what to tell them. The two either genuinely didn't know these curse words, or were taunting her like an outcast.

"Well, lady?"

"Ask your father what he means. Those are his words."

"Come on, you strumpet, did you get your quim jabbed?"

He began to laugh along with the other. "You a cherry? Take to your back for a greenback?"

The turn of the boys brought fear to her heart. The faces of the town turned villainous. Those looks were stares passing judgment. She felt the moment flash into danger.

"Get away from me, you little bootlickers," Linnea said. She picked up her speed.

"Oh! This one has spirit!" he gawked.

Linnea continued her walk at a brisk pace making the fastest way to the Baxters. Her heart raced. The insult and worry spurred speed. She ignored the foul language and cat calls to the end of the block where the boys gave up the chase. By the time she was up the porch steps and through the door, Linnea was in tears.

"Child, what happened?" Mrs. Baxter called out.

Up in her room, Linnea buried her head in the pillow. This is why there was a plan. This was why R.F. had to consider his family name. She had become a strumpet.

A rap at the door was followed by Mr. Baxter, who entered and sat on the bedside. Linnea repeated what the boys had said. His face turned sad as she described how she had been treated. Deep in thought, Mr. Baxter stood, leaving her to be. She could hear him go down the stairs and start a quiet consultation with Mrs. Baxter.

A moment later, Mrs. Baxter called from the foot of the stairs, "Linnea, could we please have a word with you?"

CHAPTER 16

"*L*innea, we think it's time," Mr. Baxter started. "We are forever grateful for Baby. He's such a fine, healthy bundle."

"Those gossips," Mrs. Baxter interrupted. "You see, we live in this town. Mr. Baxter works at the college. There is a reputation we have to keep."

"And we are forever grateful."

"You said that." Linnea took a deep breath and held it a moment. She could still feel the glow from the chase. Linnea latched on to the safety of her braided hair, and began to twirl the tip out of nervousness. *People always lead you up a ramp of kindness before pushing you off with bad news.*

"I don't like it. Not one bit." Mr. Baxter started pacing the room. "You are a delightful girl, we've... I've grown fond of you, like you were my own daughter. Still, my position, salary– these can be lost."

"You don't need to explain," Linnea's voice cracked. "Those two boys opened my eyes to my reality. I was a fool to imagine anything different. I was a fool to hope there would be…" Her voice trailed off.

Mr. Baxter stepped to the roller desk and took an elegant box from the locked far left drawer. The box was beautiful, smaller than the cigar box at the general store. It had a lock with a key. He handed it to Linnea. "That's five hundred dollars in gold coins."

The box had weight, the construction a purpose. It reminded her of the bobbin boxes.

"More than a year's wage we saved and squirreled away, Linnea. We want you to take this money and start a new life."

"The Settlement" she said to herself.

"Pardon?"

This time she said it outloud. "The settlement. It was R.F.'s plan."

Mr. Baxter nudged Mrs. Baxter, saying in a low voice, "Give it to her."

"Linnea," Mrs. Baxter said as she pulled a piece of paper from her pocket, "this came in the post for you. I opened it and read it. That was wrong of me. It's a letter from R.F. to you."

Hope stirred in her heart again. "He did think of me!" Trembling, she took the letter and began to read.

Her heart felt like it stopped as she read. The blood

drained from her face. She looked to Mrs. Baxter and back to the letter.

"You are a smart and wonderful young lady, Linnea." Mrs. Baxter wrapped her warm hands around Linnea's shaking ones. "You can do anything you want. Go anywhere you choose. The decision is yours."

"You could go west and homestead," suggested Mr. Baxter. "Or to a city if you enjoy the work. It's your choice."

MR. BAXTER WALKED Linnea to the iron works where the coach would take her to Jackson. Mrs. Baxter had given her a suitcase along with several of the outfits Linnea had liked most. The three exchanged pleasantries at the house to save the scene from prying eyes.

Linnea thought Mr. Baxter looked sad to see her go as he watched as the coachman loaded her case. "Where will you go?" he asked.

"First, I will go to Jackson for the train."

"And from there?"

"There's no one for me in Detroit. The world continues to grow. I don't know. I don't know."

1862 - 1863

BOOK II

1862 - 1863

CHAPTER 17

Soot and cinder scarred the brick holes where the windows once sat. Linnea could see all the way through the emptiness of the textile mill to the rear wall against the rail yard. The burnt remains of the machine sat between the once parallel but now warped and twisted tracks where her whole world had been pushing that cart back and forth. Months after the accident, the distinct smell of death lingered over the ghostly remains of the place that had been so busy, full of productivity and life.

"Our fortunes have changed," R.F. 's letter had started. An understatement if there ever was one. The letter went on to explain what had happened during the coldest of winter nights to keep the dormitory warm, how fast the fire spread, and the lives extinguished in flames that night when one gas lamp wasn't snuffed out. "Now I must return, back to Father, back to the east, to rebuild the family name."

During the coach ride to Jackson, looking out the window of the train on return, there was a single thought of gratitude circling in her head. She was fortunate. She survived. Going away had allowed her to stay alive. But now what use was she?

A qualm of despair overcame Linnea. "To be of use again."

The street seemed familiar in many ways. Aside from the foreign landscape created by the former factory, she would have thought this another normal afternoon. She walked six blocks to the Fifth Ward where the Blindbury Hotel stood near Cass Park. Single horses and coaches filled the block from end to end in a line waiting to carry guests across the city. For some time she stood unnoticed, watching drivers. She needed to find a room for the night. She had never done this before, and had no idea where to begin.

Linnea watched the hotel with patience. She saw that when guests stepped down from the coach, there were attendants from the hotel to help with the luggage. The intimidating man at the door only acted like a statue until the door needed opening. Then his service went into action. Through the front window she could see there was a desk and the desk had staff that guests would speak with before walking up the grand staircase off the lounge. She could do all these things; she needed only the spirit to act like she belonged.

The statue man gave her an odd look at first, but eventually opened the door. The lobby smelled like lovely flowers in bloom on a full spring day. The dark woods of the walls and the rich reds of the furniture were comforting. Maybe she didn't need a room; she could stay here in the lobby and rest. Finding courage, she approached the front desk.

"Good afternoon," she said as she approached the desk. "I am in need of a room for the night. My train home to Pontiac connects here in Detroit, and it won't leave until the morning."

The man's look of doubt was met by her stiffened spine and expectation of getting what was asked. His eyes explored the lobby, "Are you here with family? Where is your father?"

"I only need a standard room for myself, please."

Expecting this request to be a test or cruel prank, he scrutinized the lobby and the staff of the Blindbury again. Everything seemed normal.

"One room? For yourself? That would be one dollar seventy-five. Do you have one dollar seventy-five?"

"Do you accept greenbacks?"

"Yes."

Linnea began to root through her pockets and bags. She knew each moment in delay to present the currency raised the doubt she would be able to deliver what was needed. Additional pressure built as a couple stood impatiently in line behind her, waiting for service.

"I know it's here."

"Young miss, I will ask you to step aside so I may assist the next guest."

"I have it, I do."

"Miss." His voice was assertive.

"Mr. Polkemust." The authoritative voice called from behind the desk.

"Yes, Mr. Blindbury."

"Is there an issue?"

"No sir, I was aiding…"

"Here, here!" Her hand shot in the air with the folded green bill pinched between two fingers. "The smallest denomination I have is ten dollars. Will you accept that?"

The two men behind the counter looked at each other, and then at her.

"Young miss," Mr. Blindbury said. "Please join me at the far end of the counter. Mr. Polkemust, please help our next guests."

Linnea did as instructed and joined the owner.

"What are your intentions at my establishment?"

"I need a room for the night. In the morning I am taking the next train north to Pontiac. There was no direct line today from Jackson. The morning–that is when the next train is available. I don't wish to sleep on the streets."

"I see. And you are here without family? Without your father, or a brother? Is that correct?"

"Correct."

Mr. Blindbury stepped back to Mr. Polkemust, taking the black leather book from the counter, looking over the registry. "Miss, may I have a name please?"

"Linnea Karlsson."

"Karlsson with a K?"

"Yes, Linnea Karlsson, with a K." She held forward the ten dollars wishing he would take it, confirm she had a room, and allow her to stay and be treated normally.

With a scribble from the ink pen, the owner looked back up and took the money from her desperate hand. "One moment." He returned a few moments later counting out the eight and two-bits change. He handed her a key attached to an ivory carved, diamond-shaped chit, the number 1108 engraved on it. "If you would be kind enough, Linnea, to wait on that couch," he pointed to the comfortable seating, "I will have a porter take you to your room. Will you require anything else?"

"No, no. That seat?"

"Yes."

She had done it. Her perseverance paid off. Observation and imitation allowed her to seem normal enough. Though it may also have been the money.

The red couch was as comfortable and soft as it looked. She might sit here all day given the chance. The excitement of watching people come and go reminded her of Sundays in the park, watching the women in large hats be escorted. The only difference was here they wore smaller hats.

"They give you a difficult time because you're a woman." The uninvited comment came from the woman on the far end of the Davenport. She was mature, dressed in all black.

"Pardon me?"

"You are a woman, so they think less of you. And as a woman not of age, they think even less."

"I'm sure I don't know what you mean."

"Clearly you had the funds and the need for service, but they questioned you because you are a woman. You cannot vote for or against Mr. Lincoln. Once married, and you will one day succumb to the pressure and marry, you will not own property. It will all belong to your husband. Be sure to marry a good man."

"You speak bluntly."

"I speak the truth. My whole life I have seen what these men do. They fight for the black man to be free, yet ignore me."

"It must not be personal, I am sure."

"Personal or not, I am forced to abide by laws I have no voice to change. You take care to learn this lesson early, my dear. You are smarter than they give you credit for and better than what they *allow* you to do. You are your own person. Once married, you become invisible, and in the eyes of the law, less than nothing, Linnea"

"How did you know my name?"

"You are not quiet, child. Be careful with your money. There are people who would kill you for eight and two bits. They will take your money. Be sure to lock your door, hold it tight."

"Thank you. I will. I most certainly will." Linnea could feel her body start to clench in fear. She had not realized what a dangerous world she was in until now.

CHAPTER 18

*E*verything Linnea owned, anything that was "hers," lay on that bed, allowing her to assess her life. What little else she had ever owned had been abandoned or sold. Three floral dresses, one solid blue, given to her from Ellen Baxter; unmentionables; the letter from R.F.; a scrap of wax paper; a pair of dress shoes; a math book given to her as a present in Hillsdale. The box of coins. The carrying bag that all these items fit in. A coat in the wardrobe. In her pocket she still held on to the headscarf she wore in the last days of the textile. It was the last thing R.F. had seen her in, the last thing he had touched, the one thing that had been with her the longest. When her finger tips tickled at the cloth tucked in her pocket, away from anyone's eyes, it reminded her of where she had come from to get to this point, leaving her family, giving up her baby boy.

Her feelings were mixed at that moment. She was sad to have given up Baby, disappointed the Baxter's would not keep her on, and heartbroken to know that all those she knew at the textile met a fiery fate. She was proud of herself for standing up and getting this room in the hotel. Linnea was happy at the prospect of going home, where her heart was drawn to Mama and Papa. Still, she was worried about how they might receive her, never having sent word after sending her away.

She had made up her mind since she boarded the carriage in Hillsdale to purchase a ticket to Pontiac, wanting to see Mama and Papa. Linnea wasn't sure if they wanted to see her. Would they expect her to come home when the textile had burned down? Did they think she was one of the dead? Were they even still on the farm?

After a night's rest in the comfortable bed, she bathed and found breakfast. She checked out of the room, giving compliments to the staff and thanking Mr. Blindbury for the stay. Skipping the coach line, she carried her case twelve blocks to the train station and arrived with time to spare.

Sitting on a bench, the light of day felt warm on her face. She was glad to have the days grow longer again. The time for planting and birthing on the farm would be here soon enough. Maybe that would be how she could be of use.

"Excuse me?" a gentle voice said.

She looked up to see a familiar face. The young man from the postal car. He looked the same as when they shared a look in Jackson.

"You are the girl I brought to Detroit, are you not?"

She smiled. "I am. You are the young man who took me to the textile mill."

"I had feared you might have perished in the blaze, but held hope that you might be in Jackson."

"Yes, I was."

"It was you! You were that girl on the platform. Where are you going today?"

"Back to Pontiac."

"You wouldn't care to ride in the postal car with me again, would you? It can get rather lonesome there between stops."

"I-"

"That's good, you purchased a ticket, you have a comfortable seat, and I can only offer you a bag of mail to sit on."

"I- I would," she replied. "I think on that ride to Detroit often. It was a memorable day."

"I saw you across the platform and thought to take the opportunity and see if it was you."

"It is. It is me."

"You will?"

"Yes, I will ride with you."

He offered his elbow, a first for her. In imitation of the large hatted women in the park, she placed her hand on top and walked two steps before realizing her case remained behind.

"Let me get that," he offered.

The train car was like she remembered. The open door,

rocking lamp, and the comforting rhythms of the rail. This man was handsome in a different way than R.F., with more brawn in his chest and thicker arms from all his labor. He was missing a mustache. Nearly all of the men found this fashionable. But not him. Would it matter that he was ten years older than her? It hadn't mattered to her that R.F. was at least that much older.

"I apologize, but I don't know your name. In my mind, you are the man in the uniform from that day."

"Hiram."

"It's a pleasure to meet you, Hiram. I'm-"

"Linnea. I know your name. It was on your delivery form."

"Have you ever had any other deliveries like that one? A Penny Black stamp child?"

"You were the first I have ever had the pleasure to know."

"Would you do that again?"

"I reflected often on that day, and you, and what I had done for the half dollar. Frequently, when stopping through Detroit, I would trace those steps hoping to see you again, see what became of you. Had I delivered you into the hands of a disreputable rascal? Had I ruined your life? I never knew."

"That you took the delivery, this is what always caused me to wonder."

"Not something I take pride in. I am glad to see you are well."

The Michigan spring had started to bloom that week,

transforming the mud and yellow remains of last year's grass, wet with melted snow, to the pale green buds above and deeper green blades of grass below. The farms she passed didn't have the children running with the train to try and keep pace, but the plow and horse were drawing long lines across the landscape to prepare to seed.

Hiram explained his route as they rode along through the countryside. In tandem with another carrier, the two rotated the lines between Pontiac, Detroit, Jackson, Battle Creek, Kalamazoo, Gary, Indiana, and Chicago with all the small stops between. In Chicago they transferred the post to the "fast mail" by barge and paddle boats south, or to the new train lines being built running to far western territories. The new lines would get up to twenty-five miles per hour.

To Linnea, the idea of travel seemed like a romantic adventure. Hiram admitted no two days were the same; however, all were spent in this single mail car.

When they reached Pontiac, Hiram delayed his duties at the platform while exchanging pleasantries. Unable to keep the train waiting longer, he completed his tasks, and signaled to the engineer.

Linnea enjoyed the exchange and watched him rush to load the new mail bags and ride away with a final wave from the open car door. She knew he would be back four days each week, at roughly this hour of the day.

Walking the familiar two track road that passed the family farm, the chipping drum of the downy woodpecker stopped. It called out the early spring excitement in a string of hoarse, high-pitched notes. She didn't know how much she had missed the notes of home until now. In a few more steps the incessant chirrup of the friendly house sparrow greeted her, giving her wings, speeding her steps to the clearing where the road passed home.

Rounding the great tree at the woods edge, the open land was as she remembered. The house made by Papa's hand, the barn where she left it, and Horse, whom she had brushed and bridled, dipping his long neck to the grass. His large dark eye blinked. Raising his head and turning in recognition, he walked to her. Linnea met Horse half way as he remembered her. His long face nuzzled and butted her in welcome. Linnea walked to the house, Horse following close at her side. She could feel the butterflies in her stomach flutter more with each step. She hoped for joy, and readied her mind for despair.

Questions whirled in her head repeating the same questions. Would Mama and Papa be pleased to see her? Why didn't they write her back? Were they ashamed or disappointed? Would they take her back after being sent to the city? Would they even recognize her after all this time? What would she say? What would they say?

The sound of hammer on nail grew louder as she and Horse came round the corner of the barn. There was Papa, working away in overalls, beads of perspiration on his brow. He looked up, and their eyes connected. He recognized her.

CHAPTER 19

A thud came from the iron hammer hitting the earth when Papa dropped it. As he stepped forward to greet Linnea, his face brightened and began to glow in a way she had never known. Each step came faster until she was firmly fastened in his strong arms, swaying in embrace.

"Too tight," Linnea squeaked. "Too tight." It felt like he might never let her go.

"Mama! Mama!" He called. "Come fast, our daughter is home. Mama!"

Linnea could hear the familiar creak of the unfixed door opening followed by the wonderful voice of her mother calling out, "Linnea! Linnea!" Linnea and her father watched Mama move faster than she ever had before, each leg pumping under the housecoat and apron. The four embraced and huddled together, Mama, Papa, Linnea, and Horse.

Overjoyed with the welcome of home and heart, captured in an embrace she wished would never end, she took a breath and asked, "Where are the boys?"

Mama and Papa finally let go, and stepped back, Mama wiping a tear of joy away, "Oh Linnea. Linnea, my Linnea."

Papa, lips pursed, tried to hold back feelings. "Oh, Linnea, our Linnea."

"The boys?"

She could see in their faces the news was not good.

"Abell went to fight for the Union. And you know your brother Erik, couldn't ever leave Abell's side, followed him. Lars went west. He wanted to start to make his own way."

"And Karl? Where is Karl?"

"Oh, Linnea. It is good to see you."

"Papa! Karl?"

Papa hung his head. "We buried your brother Karl before the winter. He cut himself badly, and got sick. When he finally told us about it, it was poison in the blood."

The sadness spoiled the moment. She wished she hadn't been insistent asking. She wanted to go back to the embrace, the nuzzle from Horse poking his head between Mama and Papa, wanting a part of the attention. There was no going back, only going forward. Linnea thought to herself about the equation she had been trying to solve since meeting the blind man in Detroit. There were truth and lies, there was also life and death, and with joyful moments, there would be equally sad ones.

"You must be hungry," Mama said. "Come, I will make you your favorite."

Home looked and smelled as she remembered, with Mama's pot in the fire, Papa's pinch of tobacco, and the woody scent lingering on the timber walls. Stories poured out of her parents, one after the other. They finished each other's stories, debated the details, corrected the names of each player, it was awash with the time she had been gone. Mama didn't miss a step as she prepared food and told tales, at times holding her good knife pointed out to tell her stories. Her pancakes smelled delicious. With her strong wrist, she whipped the cast iron pan up in a swift movement flipping the cake to the other side. Golden side up, the edges of dough side down began to sizzle in lard. She took the cloth from the top of the butter bowl and set it on the table. Linnea realized in that moment how good her life had been here.

After supper, she asked, "Did you get my letters?"

"Sure, sure. They are over there."

Linnea stood to get a closer look at the pile. "These are open. Did you read them? Why didn't you write back?"

Sweetly, Mama explained, "We got them after the boys were gone, and you wrote them in English."

"We took out the ten dollars each month. Your work kept this farm sound. It kept Horse fed, seed for growing, and paid for the stone for Karl's grave."

"You were missed. You helped much more than you could know."

"Don't look sad, Linnea," Papa said. "Read them to us now. Tell us your stories. We want to hear about you."

She took the pile back to the table and pulled the oldest one from the bottom. Linnea began to read out loud the tales of the textile, the people, Ms. Stitch, the machine, her cart, and how important her job was. In one letter she explained that the phrase "kiss of death" was a charm people would take for good luck as they kissed something called a shuttle-cock. It was an important tool in the textile mill, but it could be dangerous, could hurt and kill people. By physically kissing the wooden object before putting it in the machine, you would bring good luck.

Linnea was so happy to relive these memories. She had forgotten most and appreciated that these important moments were captured here for her to remember. She felt happy and sad at the same time. For each of the faces that came back to her in the letters she also remembered that they had nearly all perished in the fire.

"I like the story about the animal, the hippopotamus," Papa said.

"They were all good. You liked the classes, and what was the man's name? R.F.?"

"Those were his initials, Mama. Rhett Fox Slater."

"Yes, R.F. What became of him? Why did your letters stop? We got the ten-dollars the last several months. No letter."

Linnea thought hard for a moment. There was the truth Mama and Papa raised her to tell, but there was also the white lie that seemed to smooth things over that she learned about from Mrs. Baxter. This would be the moment she needed to confess the truth to her family or bare the burden on her own, knowing it was something she alone would carry.

"There was an accident at the textile mill. There was a gas fire. It burnt to the ground. Many people I knew died."

"But you were spared? How did you escape?"

"I-" Linnea started the explanation but thought better of it. No matter how much she loved them and they, her, what she did, the truth, would change things forever. Better for them to know R.F. as a good man, which he was. Her affection for him, mistaken as love, was childish and not real. This was a mistake they would never need to know about. It hurt to keep silent, similar to her time in Hillsdale, the deep pain she carried from giving up her boy. Maybe one day she would tell them, but not this day. Like the moment she lost earlier by asking after Karl, she wished this memory with her parents would go untarnished and last as long as possible so as to soak in this positive light. "I was staying with friends that night. Some of the women had a room away from the dormitory, and they let me stay with them on occasion."

"How fortunate to stay that night of all nights." Mama floated through the house with happiness for her daughter's return. It was like a refreshing spring rain returned to open flowers for bees to do their business all season. A new cycle of life started.

"Yes, Mama. I was fortunate. I lost many friends. Even the new water truck the fire team purchased that summer couldn't put out the blaze."

"You will sleep in the loft," Papa said. "It is all yours now. And you will sleep tight tonight. Mama and I will put out all the lights, and you will sleep safe in your home."

Home. The word brought serenity. Papa's words brought comfort. No matter her troubles or tribulations, she was safe, protected, and loved. She was home.

CHAPTER 20

*L*innea woke when it was still dark, stiff from her first night back in the loft. The beds and mattresses had been a real luxury in her adventures, and the straw filling was unforgiving between the plank floor and her back. Linnea laughed as she thought of Abell, who was one to leap from the loft. Linnea was sensible that morning, backing down the ladder.

Her first stop was the barn. She found the oats and gave Horse a full scoop along with fresh hay. The same old brush was where she left it. She took time to whisper to Horse, telling him how good he was, what good work he had done, and to care for Papa in the field. Her brush followed the muscles of Horse and groomed his hairs. His big glassy eye blinked with its long lashes, which she interpreted as best he could accomplish for a loving return.

Chickens and egg collection were next on her list. There were eight good eggs she collected. All the hens clucked and head-bobbed happiness as their water and food dishes were filled. The rooster strutted to oversee his domain and finally gave his first cock-a-doodle-doo of the day. In a second crow, he sounded "ki-kiri-ki."

"You're getting old, rooster," Linnea scolded, "sleeping this late in the day."

Linnea delivered the eggs to the kitchen for Mama and caught her parents getting ready for the day. Mama, first out of the bed, was in the kitchen tying the strings of her apron and lighting the stove from the wood she had set the night before.

Once Papa was up, Linnea told him that Horse was fed and brushed, the eggs collected and chickens fed.

"What am I left to do?"

"You have a full day, Papa," Mama said. "You always have a full day ahead."

AT DAYBREAK, Linnea walked into Pontiac. It wasn't that long ago she would have needed permission or to find a brother to escort her. Living in the city had taught her independence. She had no lack of confidence to pursue her interests.

On the edge of the city, she passed Duncan's Tavern, where the last of the night's indulgences were being carried out the door and dropped into the muddy path of the road. The barkeep tipped his hat at her passing and brushed away the dirt from his red and white striped sleeves.

Pontiac had become an official city in her absence. There had always been talk of it when she was young. It finally happened. The sights and sounds reminded her of being in Detroit the year prior. A two horse buckboard wagon filled with goods under a tarp passed with a trop-trop-trop-trop. Pike street was busy. Grainy aromas from the flour mill caused her to sneeze when she stopped along the mill pond bridge. Peaking over rooftops, she could see the tower of the new county building.

There were three stops she had in mind to make. First the general store, next the Pontiac Weekly Gazette, and finally the butcher shop. If she happened to be near the train station at half past two, she would be on the platform.

***

A worried Mama and Papa heard the buckboard wagon before they saw it. At nearly time for supper they had no idea where Linnea would be. Yet there she was, sitting on a delivery wagon next to the son of Mr. Davis.

He pulled the horses right up to the house and tipped his hat after applying the break. His sleeves rolled past the elbow, he jumped down from the seat and helped Linnea down. Mama and Papa watched her instruct the man as he removed a bed and mattress and carried the parts into the house. Peeking in the window, they could see him carry it to the loft where he assembled it. Next he removed a wood crate from the buckboard and left it on the porch. Finally, he removed a full sack of oats and put it on the shelf in the barn.

Like imprinted baby ducks, the parents followed the Davis boy across the farm as Linnea gave her instructions, watching him deliver the goods Linnea purchased.

At the end of the delivery, she gave him money, and she was given a tip of the hat with a "thank you". Climbing into the buckboard seat, he snapped the straps and made a clicking noise, taking the crew back to the road and past the big old tree at the farm's edge.

"So much excitement, Linnea." Mama said.

"Where did you find such a fortune?" Papa asked.

Linnea, calm and patient, answered questions as best she could. She explained that there was the money sent home from the textile, there was the money that paid for her stay, but there was still some that found its way into her pocket each month. And that was money she had saved for such things.

"Did you know," Linnea asked over dinner, "that Pontiac is a city now?"

They did not.

"In town, they call this the Karlson Vid Sjon. The Karlson farm by Mud Lake. Did you know that they call that Mud Lake beyond the trees?"

When there was no answer, Linnea asked one more question. "Would you like me to read the newspaper to you?"

Papa's eyes grew wide, "Yes. Very much."

"Good. Now we have a plan for tonight."

CHAPTER 21

*H*iram and the train never arrived on that March day in 1863. Linnea walked home with worry on her mind. She could imagine that she may have mixed up the days she could see Hiram. That maybe it was his day off or he was on a different route. That could happen, maybe even was likely, but the train– The train had never failed to arrive before.

It wasn't until Monday's Detroit Free Press arrived at the news stand that she discovered why. She did not like this paper and avoided its inflammatory headlines against the abolitionists. Still, she purchased the edition and returned home to read it to Mama and Papa.

"I don't understand," Mama said. "They burned the buildings? They had a riot?"

"Conscription," Linnea explained, "is when the government forces the men to join the army. If Abell and Erik had not joined the 1st Michigan Infantry Regiment, conscription would force them to join the 14th Regiment today."

"Is this why they are upset?"

"It's the second part, called substitution, that they disagree with. If a man pays three hundred dollars, he can stay home and send a substitute in his place."

"Three hundred dollars is a lot of money. It would take years to save."

"If you wanted to keep Abell and Erik out of the war, it would have been six hundred dollars. To keep Karl and Lars from fighting, you would have paid twelve hundred."

"Who could pay that kind of money? That's outrageous!"

"That is why these people are mad, Papa. That is why Detroit faced a riot. The men I worked with at the textile mill never made that much. They would have been forced to go fight the rebels. They had to rise up and make their point."

"Never mind," Mama said. "The abolitionists are right, Mr. Lincoln is right. If slavery ain't wrong, nothing is. Our boys did right."

Papa nodded his head. "Bad luck seems to follow."

Mama sounded a harumph to affirm.

"I don't understand, Papa,. How did back luck follow?"

"Mama and I, we came to America because of the promise."

"What promise was that?"

"My Papa, Mama's Papa, they both fought the Russians when they were young. We came to America to put the wars behind us. It's like, what did you call it, substitution? People with money have a different set of rules. We left that behind, I thought. All the death, the loss, for what? One king wants something, another king wants it, and they go to war. What do they call it now, Mama?"

"Finland."

"Let them have it! How different can one king be than another? And Napoleon with Norway, all fighting and war."

"Then the famine."

"Oh, so much death. Everyone was hungry in the old country. It didn't matter which king was your king, they still couldn't feed everyone. Mama's brother, which brother?"

"Avil."

"Avil writes to the family. He had gone to America in '47. He writes that there is gold in the hills and rivers, you have to find it. He writes that there are jobs. He writes there is no king. Mama, Abell, Erik, Karl and me got on a boat to a place called Halifax in Canada."

"Your brother Lars was born in Canada," Mama added.

"That's right, Lars was born in Canada, and you were born here, Linnea. You are our true American."

"I never knew any of this."

"Sure, sure, it's in the bible we have." Mama wiped her hands on the apron and went to the chest in their bedroom. She returned with a leather book, well-read and soft. "Look inside, you'll see."

Linnea opened the book to see carefully printed names of

her family with dates and locations next to them. "Who is Anna?"

"She didn't survive."

"Would she have been my sister?"

"Yes. She was between Abell and Erik. She got sick."

Linnea nodded, and continued to look through the bible. "It would have been nice to have a sister. This is a Lutheran bible. Are we Lutherans?"

Linnea caught a look between Mama and Papa. She knew that look. That look was made when the boys asked questions Papa or Mama didn't want to answer, or didn't know how to answer.

"Sure, sure. Every good Swede is a Lutheran," Papa said.

Mama added, "Lutheran is what the king decreed my whole life."

"You had to be?"

"Sure, sure," Papa said. "That's all in the past. You get to choose what you want, Linnea. You are a true American. In America, you can be whoever you want. That's why we came here, made our declaration."

Linnea, finished with the bible, closed it, and pushed it forward on the table for Mama.

"Do you know what you want to be, Linnea?" Papa asked.

"I know what I don't want to be. The more new things I try, the list of things I *don't* want to be grows longer."

"That's our girl," said Mama. "Brave American, trying new things. Like the time you bought your bed. We had no idea you could get things delivered."

"You never leave the farm, Mama. Papa, you go to the city, what? Maybe three, four times a year? And I am going most days. There is much there, many people, and new things to try."

Papa shrugged his shoulders. "We like the farm. The farm has been good to us."

"Yes, the farm has been good to all of us."

CHAPTER 22

"*H*iram, is that you? Are you hiding from me?" she called inside the mail car. "I can see you in the corner. Did I do something wrong?"

The second postal carrier continued about his business unloading sacks from the car, until asking, "You Linnea?"

"Yes."

"He talks about you all the time. You did nothing wrong, ma'am. He's, well, different now. That's all."

"Hiram, please talk to me. You only have a few moments before the train departs."

The shadowy figure stood in the corner and stepped forward to the edge of the light coming through the barred window. Hiram, once a young handsome man, was now broken, his slouch an expression of a drained soul. The mangled and scarred skin on the right side of his face with the nearly closed and swollen eye were clear evidence confirming rumors of the Detroit riots' direct impact. Linnea could almost make out the details.

"You won't want to see me." He stepped back into the darkness.

"Please, please come closer, I want to see you. Tell me what's happened. I want to know you are whole."

"Ma'am, he was caught in the riot. He stopped the mob from killing two men, but they turned on him, letting the other two get away. Those two owe him their lives, the damned fool. My apologies."

"I know curses well, sir. No need to refrain on my behalf. Hiram *is* a damned fool," she challenged.

"Postal service requires two on each car now." He turned to call into the mail car, "Hiram, come talk to the nice lady. You've been telling me about her for two weeks. You wanted to talk with her again, you said this not an hour ago."

"Hiram, it can't be that bad."

No answer.

"It's not my place, ma'am, but you might want to give him time. I will speak to him on your behalf."

"Thank you, that would be greatly appreciated."

She watched the man climb back into the car as the whistle blew. The big wheels of the locomotive cycled through the first two fast spins, gripping the sand on the rail to gain friction before moving the train cars slowly forward. As the momentum picked up and the line of cars steamed forward, she thought she caught a glimpse of Hiram looking out through the bars of the window. He was a sad prisoner in a cage of his own design. She wanted to talk with him again. The quick talks they had had near daily when the train pulled into the station were greatly missed. She had hoped for more from him, and with him. He was a good man. Maybe too good, thinking of others and stepping into harm's way.

SHE CONTINUED, as she had done for months, to meet the train. Each time Linnea hoped this would be the day Hiram would come out of the shadows again. It was a rainy day in the second week of September when Linnea heard him speak again. In no uncertain terms or tone, Hiram stepped from the shadows, fully exposed in the light for Linnea.

She smiled to see his kind eyes again and with hope in her heart said his name as sweet and softly as possible.

With certitude he said, "Linnea, please stop. Do not visit me. Do not try. It hurts too much."

The words stung. She could feel the pain in her heart from the rejection. "Please, Hiram, give it time. Please."

"Stop." It was said nearly as a whisper, never wanting to leave his lips. From the height of the mail car the word picked up speed, and with gravity, landed on her heart below with the crushing weight of a lazy mule.

"Very well."

It was as simple a conversation as was ever shared. She

had been a silly girl with hope. There were no promises made, only assumptions she had made based on behavior and interpretation. It was presupposition and presumptuous to think he cared. These were feelings after all. Emotions had never done her well. Best to keep them hidden and inside. How many times would she need to learn this lesson again before it took hold? Feelings of friendship found betrayal with her co-workers at the textile mill. Fondness for R.F. and the ecstasy in physical entanglements pushed her toward aloofness, abandonment, and dejection. In the creation of a new life, a never ending connection between mother and son, she found the deepest despair in her decision to cut all ties. Standing at the station, she felt low, and questioned her purpose once again. What would it be?

"Linnea?"

She turned to see where the familiar voice came from on the platform. "Abell?"

CHAPTER 23

She realized that the tight embrace with her brother was now an effort to keep him upright. Linnea had run to Abell, wrapped her arms tightly around him, but her brother had not moved to meet her. A crutch under his arm was compensated for the missing leg. Half the arm she had expected to clutch was an empty sleeve. The Union uniform hid the changes the war had made on the young man.

"Abell!" She caught him from the fall and steadied him on the crutch. "Abell it is good to see you. You look all grown, this beard makes you look like Papa. I can't tell under all that fuzz if you are smiling."

"It is good to see you, Linnea. Awfully good."

"Come, let's get you in a buggy home to see Mama and Papa."

He needed aid in walking, going down steps, and getting into the buggy. She asked how he had gotten this far unaccompanied. His only reply: "Slowly."

She could see the recognition of the unchanged farm on his face. Pontiac had grown while he was away. Not the farm. The farm was still home.

She had the buggy pull to the front of the house, as close as the driver dared, to make it easy on Abell. Mama and Papa, impatient at the buggy door, nearly carried him down from the step and held him in a tight embrace. Horse, seeing Abell, galloped at speed to see him, the nuzzle and headbutts testing the young man's strength to stand.

"I guess we know who Horse likes best," Linnea said. Her words got a look from Horse, and, not for the first time, she wondered if Horse had understood her. He turned the long head to her, giving her a quick nudge before nuzzling back to Abell.

"Whoa, whoa, boy... whoa," Abell said.

Abell got comfortable in Papa's rocking chair on the porch after a little protest of "but that's your chair, Papa."

Once Abell was settled and the buggy sent on its way, the family gathered round as Abell explained his circumstances. After drills and training, they went straight into Virginia. There was a great deal of action in the eastern theater. The number of losses made him think the Union would never win. The Confederate forces were wiley, unpredictable, and seemed to always rally for a counterattack. Abell felt to always be in fast retreat. It was August of '62 when they fought close to the Capitol, and the only route of retreat was through Washington's streets. Abell described the smoke and confusion of battle, how horrifying the random landings of shot and cannon fire were, even on a fast horse. He still saw death in his dreams from many of the encounters.

When they had arrived at Gettysburg, he had been assigned to the east field on the third day of battle. He had served under General Custer in the Michigan 1st Cavalry that day. Many on both sides thought the fight would go in favor of the Rebels again. But that third day, something changed. They had sent the South packing. Cannons from three miles away had thundered all morning, pounding at the wall in the valley. "You would think the world was ending." In the east field where he had been stationed, stood a left-over set of units who stayed to hold the road while main forces were sent to defend Maryland. "We could see the Rebels' plans play out, the signals obvious. I saw friends in Michigan 5th and 7th go into the fight and hold the line. When General Custer came to the men of the 1st, he yelled 'Come on, you wolverines!'"

"Wolverines," Papa chuckled. "There are no wolverines in Michigan."

"He called us that because he knew our reputations to fight, hold our own in a scrape. Which we did that day, and more. We gave it to 'em good."

With less enthusiasm, Abell explained the moment when things had turned for him. How the cannon shell, called a canister shot, took out the horse, his arm and leg. The one shot was made up of hundreds of grape sized pieces of metal. "If it wasn't for that horse taking most of the blow, I wouldn't be here." Later he admitted, "I was arrogant. I was too close to the cannons."

Linnea noticed that she wasn't alone in choking up. Mama and Papa shared in her tears at hearing the tale. Even when they learned how he had been recovered from the field of battle, given the best treatment by General Custer's personal surgeon, and returned home by boat and rail, there were tears, tears of sadness, tears of joy.

"We are happy you are home," Papa said.

"We have you. We are thankful to have you." Mama bent over him in the chair hugged her oldest tight, reluctant to pull away.

When she finally let go, allowing him to breathe fully, Abell sat up straight.

Mama asked, "Where is your brother Erik?"

The three hardest words to speak might be, "I don't know." In the past, the phrase could have been an admission of ignorance or a cutting response that Mama found disrespectful. For Abell, the words were filled with the bubbling guilt he had carried from the northern Virginia battle that would come to be known as Running Bull Two. The brave mask Abell held melted his manly exterior into the cries of a child. The quick breaths. The stop-start whine and words. Between the tears he explained that Erik went on to the field right behind Abell, and got lost in the rain of shot and cloud of battle filled with smoke and fire. Erik was gone. He wasn't with the dead. He wasn't on the field. He wasn't mixed with other units of the calvary or Union army. He was gone.

Mama went inside, mumbling something like, "make something to eat," but Linnea knew better. She needed to be alone. Papa removed his pipe and wanted to sit a while. Abell asked to be alone. Insisting he didn't need help, Abell took Horse to the barn, each helping the other move forward.

Linnea thought to herself, *this must be grief, how unwelcomed this feeling.*

Abell continued to spend a great deal of time in the barn upon his return. Horse had never been more pampered. He was alway being cleaned and brushed. He always had fixed shoes. He was hand fed. When Papa needed Horse in the field, Abell had to stand watch within shouting distance or Horse wouldn't work.

Looking at the ladder to the loft and the steps up the porch, Abell decided to sleep in the barn. In the still of an October night, when the wind died down Abell's voice called out his little brother's name in desperation, "Erik? Where are you? Erik?"

Linnea, stirred by these calls, got down from the loft and found herself facing the most amazing display of northern lights. The pink, green, and blue curtains of light dancing in the sky were an amazing display of wonder. It was at times like these she would think about her boy. She hoped he was happy and loved. She wondered if on a night like this he might also be awake watching the world in all its wonderment. Her heart ached to know he would not inquire about his mother. For all he knew he had a mother, and she was with him. Her child occupied a space in her heart she could never fill.

Linnea decided that her purpose would be this family. The farm needed to be run, Mama and Papa needed looking after, Abell needed a sister, and Horse needed Abell. This wasn't the family she had started with, it wasn't the family looking after her child, but it was the family she had and would care for. These were people who would not trick or taunt her. They were not the ones to seduce and abandon her, nor were they filled with shame to be connected to her.

1880 - 1881

BOOK III
1880 - 1881

CHAPTER 24

*L*innea felt herself a woman of two worlds during her walk into the city on a beautiful early spring morning of 1880. One part was of the farm, a whole world unto itself, and the other was the small city of Pontiac, where she was able to explore her independence.

On the farm was Mama, Papa, and Abell. Custer, Abell's horse that had joined the farm after Horse passed at the age of twenty-nine, was named after the general who had led Abell in the East Field push at Gettysburg and had recently died on the frontier. There was nothing quick on the farm except Custer. The days were long and slow as were the people. Papa tried to keep up with Custer by deepening the plow's cut, using the ground to act as an anchor slowing him down. Mama's wisdom shone when she could no longer catch chickens to cook for dinner. She nabbed them while they were being fed, full bellies keeping them slow.

In the city, Linnea had made a reputation of independence that other women did not carry. Pontiac was now a city of professionals. Doctors, lawyers, and businessmen were attracted to the Pontiac High School for their children's education, many of whom went on to University. Workers found full employment on the other side of town with the wool and grist mills running off the power of the Clinton river. Independent craftsmen hard at work made the city of Pontiac one of the largest producers of carriages. Detroit may have been known as the "Stove Capitol of the World," but Pontiac made some of the finest carriages.

Linnea was good with mathematics and practiced in writing, skills that set her apart. She was often seen reading. On Wednesdays, she would balance the books at Johnson's General Store, doing the same on Thursday afternoons for Sam's Drugs.

Socially, she had a few close friends, yet she had remained single. Linnea was a pretty woman, and she was chased by many men. Even when courted time and again, she resisted anything serious. Some called her a "spinster," and the phrase "old maid" had started to avail itself now that she turned 28 years of age.

Abiding Hiram's wishes, she had stopped waiting on the platform every day. Still, the days she was in the city, she seemed to always be in sight of the station from the porch of the Hotel Clinton where her view down Patterson Street went unimpeded to the mail platform. Once she had stopped waiting for him at the station, he had started to exit the mail car for his work. He grew stronger over the years, his body lean and tight, shoulders broad from lifting sacks of mail. From a safe distance, he looked like the same handsome man she had known. From this distance his smile and eyes could be made out. While it couldn't be true, each time he ended his work to part for the next destination, Linnea thought maybe he tipped his hat in her direction. From this distance, she allowed herself to believe it, even though her mind would debate that Hiram was wiping his brow from the effort. For roughly fifteen years, she felt sound and secure from the porch of Hotel Clinton.

One lovely day, during her normal walk from the farm to the city, she transformed from the slow and easy life of the farm to her independent self with each step. She heard a voice that stopped her in her tracks.

"Pardon me, Ma'am."

A worker from the crew improving the street out front of the burnt remains of the Crofoot building raised his palm with bent arm.

"Sorry, ma'am. It's for your safety," he said.

Linnea watched as the men removed the bung from a large barrel and tipped it over, letting the black thick goo of coal tar run across the packed gravel and dirt. Its momentum carried it to the walk's edge where it struck like a miniature wave on the shore, carrying the splatter where she would have been stepping.

"Don't want your pretty dress to get messed," he added.

Linnea immediately noticed his kind eyes and smooth timbre in his voice. The messy work was less interesting.

"Just another moment, ma'am."

"Linnea," she corrected.

"Pardon?"

"My name is Linnea Karlsson."

"Mrs. Karlsson, thank you for waiting."

"Miss."

"Miss Karlsson, thank you."

"And your name? It's only polite since you know mine."

He smiled at her boldness. "Lincoln. Lincoln Beaumont."

"I knew a Beaumont from Hillsdale."

"I am a Beaumont from Lansing."

"Still a good name. Are you sealing *all* the streets?"

"We are. My team is sealing all the east-west streets, there's another team doing north-south."

"I saw that carriage rail being placed on Woodward. Exciting to see our city grow."

"Yes, Miss Karlsson. Not my city, but it keeps us busy."

"You don't live in Pontiac?"

"No, ma'am. Like I said, I hail from Lansing, hired by the State. I'm passing through on the working crew."

"I've never been to Lansing. Is it as lovely as Pontiac?"

He leaned closer to speak low, "To be honest, Pontiac is much nicer, and by the judge of things, the ladies much prettier."

Linnea blushed for the first time in as long as she could

remember. "Aren't you a little young for me?" Her natural inclination tilted her head and drew her chin closer to her breast. "Well, I am sure..."

"Miss Karlsson–"

"Please, call me Linnea."

"Linnea, my apologies if this is too forward, but would you be available this week to call on?"

"Beaumont! Move it!" a worker called out from the street.

"That's the foreman. Would you be available?"

"Aren't you a little young for me?"

"What's age beside experience? I won't hold, what, two years it against you?" He winked.

"Come on, Beaumont. Get a move on."

"I will!" Lincoln called to the foreman. He turned back to Linnea. "Name the night, and we can meet at the Summit hotel. Say, six o'clock?"

In an instant Linnea shuffled in her mind the responsibilities she had for the week and decided that Thursday she could dress appropriately and she would complete the books at Sam's at about the right time. Additionally, the office above Sam's would allow her to freshen up. "Thursday."

"Stop your lollygagging, Beaumont, and get back to work!"

"Thursday? Excellent. Thursday. Six-o-clock. The Summit."

"May I pass now?"

"Absolutely, my lady, you may pass. Watch the grease." He lowered his hand and made an elegant bow, pointing her on her way. He gestured to the crowd gathering on the walk behind Linnea. "Right this way, ladies and gentleman. Watch your step!"

LINNEA'S CHEEKS were sore from smiling all day as she sat at the dinner table with her family that night. *Two years is nothing. The loves of her past were at least a decade older. Why not try slightly younger?*

Abell was the first to notice. "I don't remember seeing you smile like this for some time. What happened to you today?"

"I met a man."

"You met a man? A man in the city?" Mama asked. "What do you mean?"

"A gentleman asked to call on her, Mama," Abell explained.

"Good, good," Papa said. "Tell us about this man in the city."

"His name is Lincoln Beaumont, from Lansing."

"A Lansing man," her brother teased. "A Capitol man. Does he work for the government?"

"You could say that."

"Never trust a politician," Papa said.

"Even Mr. Lincoln? You wouldn't have trusted him?" Abell teased his father.

"Well, maybe Lincoln."

"You see his face on everything in the city," Linnea picked at her plate still thinking about Lincoln. "Cigar boxes, laundry soap, buntings and flour. Anything there is to sell has President Lincoln's face."

"Don't sway from the conversation, dear sister. What about this man you met?"

"He seems smart, has a job, and can keep a conversation going. This is all I can say."

"That's little to agree to meet with a stranger."

"I can't describe it to you better, but there was something about him."

"Maybe I should escort you into town to meet this Lincoln Beaumont?"

"Don't be silly, Abell. When was the last time you went to the city?"

"Last month. Custer and I rode to the city for a new ax head and to pick up this season's seed. Papa, they're putting in electric lines in the city to run a trolley. They are doing away with the horse-drawn omnibus. Electricity, it's going to be in every city soon enough."

"That is something," Papa said. "It's hard to imagine that in my life I've gone from that small sod house in Sweden to electricity. What wonder will they come up with next?"

"I guess if Linnea can find a man," Abell chuckled, "anything is possible!"

"That is enough," said Mama. "Don't say things like that about your sister. When was the last time you courted anyone, Abell?"

He looked to his plate, "I am sorry, Linnea, I was only teasing. I am happy you accepted, truly I am."

The tightness in her face from smiling wouldn't go away with those teasing words from Abell. She knew they came from a place of jealousy. Her smile carried her through the first half of the week. No dark thoughts or memories could spoil the hope and happiness the anticipation of their date brought. On that Thursday morning, she put on her favorite dress and added to her reticule a few items for later in that day that she wouldn't normally bring. After she fed the chickens and did chores, she helped Abell with the bridal and straps, putting Custer in the harness. The buckboard Papa and Able had built two summers earlier was fitted for Custer. Abell, once in the cart, took Linnea the mile to the new city limits of Pontiac, saying only four times, "The city keeps getting closer and closer."

Linnea noticed the clock in the square more frequently that day. It seemed to take longer than normal to pass an hour. Linnea's mind drifted at least twice in her accounting, causing her to make mistakes, one for fifty-eight cents and the other over four-hundred dollars. She shook herself as she restarted. She needed to focus on the job at hand.

Daylight was noticeably longer this week. The lights of the street started to come on as she walked over to the Summit. *Slower,* she thought to herself. *Don't be too early. Keep him waiting a little bit.*

In the shop windows along the way, President Lincoln's face appeared on more goods. It only made her think of

Lincoln Beaumont. A bar of soap, and her mind went to being stopped on the street. The cigar box, his large hand and strong arm keeping her safe from the spill. She reminded herself, *slower, don't want to show desperation.*

Stepping up to the wrapped porch of the Summit, she could see inside through the windows to the lobby as the man out front opened the door for her. The red luxurious seating took her back in time to another brave moment and the words from the woman dressed in black, "Be sure to marry a good man." Here was that moment caught in her mind from nearly two decades earlier, like the haunting refrain of a song. A good man. Would Lincoln Beaumont be that good man?

CHAPTER 25

"This rhubarb punch holds quite the kick," Linnea said.

"It's splendid, I must admit, but not as lovely as you this evening."

"Aren't you the sweet talker? I'm sure that you've said this to others."

"Linnea, you might be surprised, but I don't find myself in this situation often. This might be the first. Tell me more about you, I am fascinated to learn."

She told him about the farm, her family, and about the things she admired about her life. That she also worked surprised him, but he did not shutter.

"Do you enjoy the work?"

"I do. I've always applied myself. There is something inside of me that will not settle. I need to push for something more, never sure what it is. Life is much better when I think of it as a series of experiences gathered, and discovering the things I am not fond of, rather than driving to a single goal. But enough about me. Who is Lincoln Beaumont?"

Lincoln explained he was the only child to two wonderful parents. He had lived in Lansing all his life and been doted on by an overprotective mother and rather distant father who was more interested in books. His father had taken his turn in state politics for four years when Lincoln was young, and later tried his hand in business at a firm.

"But I want to know about you, Mr. Beaumont, not your parents."

He laughed, "I was eager to explore the world at sixteen. I was well educated but not interested in the Agricultural College, no matter how my parents pushed. I packed up my things, and two summers back I joined a working crew that had been established by the state."

"Do you enjoy the work?"

"I have seen the cities. We spent a year in Detroit after some time in Lansing. We've worked our way north here to Pontiac with a train of people following behind us."

"My father was telling us about growing up in Sweden the other night. Can you imagine? He grew up in a sod house. Do you want to stay with this working crew?"

"Lineann, at this moment I don't want to be anywhere without you."

Another blush response came to Linnea that she couldn't help or hide. Allowing herself to feel something more than fantasies since R.F. was a risk she might be willing to accept. There was something different about Lincoln Beaumont. He was not the most handsome man to show interest, nor the most charming, but there was something about him that felt right. There seemed some instant connection she could not identify or deny. Deep inside, she knew she wanted to care for him. She wanted to be with him.

Both glasses of punch empty, they moved outside to the front porch to sit a spell and watch the city life before them. They talked about the passersby as if they had rich and amazing lives rushing off to the theater for a play or some tavern to close out the night. Linnea enjoyed this little game between them, imagining the stories of couples before them in a romantic tryst, or the twisted tales of a devious man making his way through the dark streets.

She recognized the distinct clop-clop-clop of those particular horse shoes on the road. It was Custer with Abell at the reins.

"The hours have passed quickly, Lincoln. I fear that it's my brother on his way to gather me and take me home."

"I see," he said with disappointment. "May I call on you again?"

"You had better." She leaned over to him under the flutter of the gas lamp on the porch, partially covered in the flickered darkness and kissed him full on the lips. The courage it may have taken in her youth didn't matter. She knew what she wanted, and she wasn't afraid to pursue it.

He was surprised and excited to find the bold move left

him wanting more. As she drew away, she could see the longing in his eyes, and she fully expected him to call on her again.

"Linnea?" Abell called out. "Ready to go home?"

"On my way, dear brother, on my way." She smiled one last time to the young man, still tasting him on her lips, then turned and went down the steps. With a swift push of her legs she was into the seat of the buckboard next to Abell.

"Ready?"

"Yes," she said. "I am ready."

CHAPTER 26

"*I*'m exchanging our wheat for flour at Dawson's," Papa declared.

Abell raised an eyebrow at his father. "But we've always gone to Brook's."

"I was speaking with the Larrsons, and they got a better deal with Dawson. I hear tell that all the Swedes are using Dawson's."

"Well, if Mr. Larrson says Dawson's is better, I trust it. Larrscoop farm has always had success."

"He tells me that the summer will be long and the winter mild from his readings."

"Will you two save the conversation until Linneas gentleman arrives?" Mama said. "We want to make him feel welcome."

"Yes, Mama," Papa said.

Abell's smile held the dastard slant of a brother's taunt, "Did Linnea warn you two that he's a little on the young side?"

"Nothing wrong with that, Abell. Your mother is a year older than me, you know?"

"Papa! Do not spread lies now." Mama tossed her dish towel at him. "I am much younger."

Papa winked at Abell. "Yes, my love, much younger."

"Age has nothing to do with it," Mama said. "Can he provide? Will he treat her right? Those are the things that matter."

"Will you all stop talking about me as if I wasn't here?" Linnea called down from the loft. "I hear everything up here... Everything."

The quick creak of the ladder with each step sounded her hurry. "How do I look?" She turned to show them the new dress she had purchased last Saturday special for the occasion.

"You look lovely, my girl." Papa stood and kissed her cheek. "Like a dream."

"You look divine, sister. I would call on you myself."

"Don't be vile, Abell. Even if it's in good humor," Mama scolded. "You look nice. This Lincoln Beaumont will find you beautiful."

The farm normally didn't hold this type of tension and excitement. The only visitors to Vid Sjon Farm were those who had followed to America from Sweden. The community looked to Papa with respect, as having been there first and written to the homeland about all of the promises of Pontiac.

Custer's neigh gave Lincoln away. They could hear him approach the house on horseback. The Karlsson clan stopped their conversation cold when they heard Custer's warning and gave each other a look.

"Be good." Linnea's finger wagged with instruction.

Making way to the porch, the family greeted Lincoln while he wrapped his horse strap to the hitching post.

"Good looking horse you have there, Mr. Beaumont," Abell said.

"Thank you. You can all call me Lincoln."

"Named after the President were you?" Papa asked.

"I am, yes. My parents were very fond of him."

"Good man," Papa said.

"Come, come, please come in, Mr. Beaumont." Mama hurried them along.

Once inside, introduction and pleasantries continued. Linnea took Lincoln's arm with a peck to his cheek in greeting. Papa and Mama exchanged an awkward look upon seeing this side of their grown daughter. The natural progress of her life had been retarted by her time at the textile, and the lack of acceptable men her age prevented them from seeing her this way.

Papa stiffened his back. He was a little hurt, possibly jealous with the attention she had for someone else and wondered if this was normal.

Linnea could see the glow in Mama. Her cheek rosy,

smile big, and eye's bright, Mama was as sunny as a spring day. She seemed to want to dote on Lincoln as if he were one of her own.

The moment felt more casual for Abell, having met the man on many occasions and caught the two of them kissing more than once. "Lincoln," he put his good hand forward for his well-known upside down handshake. "How was the ride over? Did you find the house from the instructions?"

"Yes, it's not as far from the city as it sounded."

"It gets closer every day."

"Please, please, Mr. Beaumont, take a seat. Supper is ready for you," Mama said.

"Yes, Lincoln, why don't you sit there, next to Linnea. You can take Lars' seat."

"Lars?"

"He is my brother who's out west," Linnea explained. "The youngest of the boys."

"I don't recall you mentioning him."

"Oh, sure, sure, Lars is the frontiers man of the family." Papa said. "He made the land rush, few years back, and now has more than a hundred head of cattle. He writes to Mama monthly."

"How splendid," Lincoln said.

Mama was generous to the new boy at the table, serving him the best cut from the roast and an extra half potato.

"Too much, Mrs. Karrlson! Thank you."

"What is it you do?" Papa asked.

"Well, I had been on a working crew these last few years,

paving the streets. On meeting your daughter, I gained employment at the Eastern Michigan Asylum as an associate administrator."

"At the asylum for the insane? That must be dangerous work."

"No. As an administrator, we look after the patient's care and provide the best treatment available."

Linnea raised her chin. "Lincoln's a smart man."

"They have special quarters for you at the asylum?" Papa asked.

"I have a room there at the moment."

"Eat. Eat," Mama said.

"This is delicious, Mrs. Karrlson, thank you."

"Such a polite boy." Mama pointed to Papa and Abell. "You two could learn a lesson."

Big conversations about small things continued through the dinner. Lincoln fit in naturally with the family rhythms. At times, Lincoln looked to Linnea for help on Swedish slang or a misheard word. When the men retired to the porch with tobacco, Lincoln began to explain the reason for his presence that night.

"Mr. Karrlson, I am here to ask for your daughter's hand in marriage. She and I have been talking it over, and we think it's the right thing."

Papa puffed on his pipe. "You've only known her two months. Are you certain of this?"

"I am. I love Linnea very much. She makes me feel whole.

She fills something in me that I have thought my life was missing."

"Sure, sure, I felt the same about Mama. Are you able to care for her? Protect her?"

"Yes. I am financially secure, have no debts, and am fully employed with the possibility of advancement."

Papa puffed again, thinking, then asked, "Where would you live? In a room at the asylum? That doesn't seem right."

"We are looking at property outside of town."

"Sure, sure, makes sense. City can be expensive. Are you taking her far away?"

"No, sir, it's the property across the road from you. You will still see her every day. She wants to stay here."

"Across the way?"

Linnea came through the door interrupting the conversation she had been listening to just steps away. "Yes, Papa, across the way."

"You want to buy land from Larrson? Where will you get the money?"

"Papa, I've been saving for years for the occasion."

"I'll say!" Lincoln said. "Your daughter had a box of gold coins squirreled away. Bought the land out-right."

There was a pause in the conversation as Papa and Abell looked at Linnea with awe.

She gulped. It suddenly felt very warm in the single bedroom house. A glow started to form on Linnea's brow. Too many opportunities had passed leading to this moment to tell everyone the whole truth. The omission, the white lie, the secret past, this original sin of disobedience, loomed over her head like the sword of Damocles. She was caught and would have to explain in detail. There was a small tickle of relief in her heart to relieve the burden. Linnea thought to herself, *I was young. I made mistakes.* They loved her and would understand.

Papa broke the silence, asking Lincoln, "If you're at the asylum, how will you work the land?"

"I will, Papa," Linnea blurted out. "I take good care of this place, and a few more acres will help bring more from the harvest."

Papa's brow was furrowed at the news coming to him so fast. "I don't think you came here to ask me for her hand, but to tell me her hand is taken."

"Papa." Linnea kneeled by his side, taking his hand in hers on his lap. "You are not going to lose your little girl. I am going to be right across the road. Lincoln is a good man. Give us your blessing."

Papa looked to Abell, "Did you know?"

"I suspected."

"Mama? Were you in on this?"

Mama, ear at the door, peeked out and said, "You say 'yes,' Papa. She loves him."

"Sure, sure. Who am I to stand in the way of love?"

CHAPTER 27

A simple wedding was held on the Fourth of July. All of the local Swedish families joined them on the farm. As bride and groom Linnea and Lincoln walked down an aisle between the guests. In front of all the witnesses they exchanged vows, and the priest confirmed the union announcing, "You may all kiss the bride." The laughter and love continued into a reception where a spit cake was made for dessert on an open spit fire, along with fresh lamb and beef with the sweet sauces from recipes they brought from the home land.

Speeches began once the glasses of courage had been poured. Larrson wished them a long life of happiness. Andersson followed with a story about a goat. Johannson reminded them all about the famine way back when and that the only way they made it through was together.

Papa, a little drunk and a bit sad, started, "Thank you all for being here on this beautiful day to celebrate Linnea and Lincoln. And to celebrate this great new country we call home. Many of you have asked me these last weeks, 'What do you think of this Beaumont boy?' After all, he's no Swede. He is not a farmer. He might not know which end of a cow to milk. You've never seen him plow a field or build an outhouse. And I will tell him now what I've told you each time you ask. If I had to search the world over to find the perfect man for my daughter, it would be Lincoln Beaumont. He is honest. He is hardworking. He is kind. He treats Linnea well. Most of all, he loves my Linnea. Lincoln, Linnea, here is to you. Make your mother and I happy– go make many grandbabies to help on the farm."

His speech brought a joyful laughter of life to all the friends and family in the community that day. Papa had reminded everyone what they all valued, what brought them to this point, and the continuation of that growth through generations.

Linnea had never looked this beautiful. Many of the men commented on how lucky Lincoln was and began to call him "Lucky Lincoln." After Papa's speech the spit cake was served, and as the long July day turned to evening, fireworks began to shoot off in honor of all that was grand about that day and the country that allowed for it all to happen.

Abell, who had brought out his Union uniform for the occasion, spent the day paired off with Anna Olson. Linnea overheard Mama make mention to Papa that she had never known Abell to spend that much time talking with anyone outside of the house. The man of few words found many that day for Anna. It didn't come to mind that she was thirteen years his junior. That's how things were after the war of rebellion. So many men lost in battle, so many lonely women left behind.

At the end of the celebrations, with buntings strung around the buggy, Lincoln and Linnea rode back to the city where they stayed at the Summit and talked about the whirlwind they had lived since that first night on the front porch at the hotel.

Lincoln made no effort to hide that he was nervous that night. He had been a virtuous man. Linnea shared the concern, as she wanted this night to be special for him. With tender talk and a shared trust with each other, everything progressed better than imagined. Her memories of the past were a mixture of pleasure and pain, quick uncertainty, and stolen moments. But here she found pleasure being with Lincoln as they were better paired. Lincoln was perfect. They put each other at ease and cherished every moment.

There would never be the right time to explain what had happened, Linnea decided. Her love and happiness were too much to risk on the truth. She never wanted to lose this feeling. She hated the idea of being alone. And the truth about R.F. alone in his office each Sunday afternoon where he made her feel so good and wanted, or the truth about the results, a baby boy delivered in Hillsdale that winter night, would only risk it all. Too much time had passed for her past to be of concern. She was ready for this life and love to carry her forward.

By the month's end they were ready to move into their newly completed house, a two story design with a porch that wrapped around all four sides. A steep stair in the front and back included safety rails. A modern stairwell at the entrance led to the second floor where a master bedroom and two additional bedroom could be found, one of which Linnea hoped to use as a nursery. Between the master bedroom and the nursery was a bathroom with indoor plumbing. The house was wired for electricity, ready for the lines to be available for connection in the area.

Once the excitement of being carried into the home by her young, strong husband had passed, she looked out the front window across the road to her childhood home. Linnea admitted to Lincoln that she was a little saddened by the view. From this vantage, it seemed like an old shack compared to her new home. She thought to herself that spending some of those earned gold coins on her parents would have been better than saving it for her own interests. And the beautiful steps up to the house, once thought wonderful, would be a chore for Abell to visit. She worried that Mama and Papa might think less of her for the indoor plumbing that only the well-to-do could afford.

The big old tree at the property's edge looked lonely where the land had been cleared for lumber and plowed for farming. Linnea could remember finding the old faces in its bark as a child. She thought of the time when she had been taken by the hand down the road on her way to Detroit, when she had passed the tree with a smile at the sweet sounds of the "coooo-OOOOO-woo-woo-woo" from the Mourning Dove, make-believing the sound was Farfar watching over her.

With a few kind words Lincoln lifted her spirits. Progress was why her family had come to America. Their "true American" was living the dream they had held onto back in the old country.

Linnea realized that once she and Lincoln settled and had children of their own, Papa would be a Farfar. Mama would have someone new to dote on. And Uncle Abell could give them rides on the back of Custer while telling them stories of the war.

"You're correct, Lincoln. This is only a new beginning, not the end."

CHAPTER 28

Summer's middle month tested the open windows at the top of the spire. August's hot and humid Michigan weather rose up the stairwell to the extra level where windows opened past the pitched roof. Ventilation breezed through the house keeping them all cool.

It was on such a Sunday when Linnea invited everyone over for Sunday Supper. Papa commented on how refreshing it was to be in the new house. Abell brought Anna Olson. The two had spent much of their free time together since the wedding.

"There never is a good time for these things," Lincoln said over dinner after making sure everyone was in the room. "Linnea and I have an announcement to make. We are going to be parents."

Mama clapped her hands together as she let loose a

squeal of pure delight. Papa was quick to his feet to slap his son-in-law on the back. Abell raised his glass in congratulations to the couple. In later years, Linnea would look back on this moment time and again. She was happy, her life was perfect with her love, family, and hope for the child on the way.

After supper, Linnea insisted that Mama enjoy the evening on the porch. She had done enough dishes in her life, and it was Linneas turn to do them. She also held tight to an ulterior reason. The sink had a window over it that looked over the farm at the back of the house. One of her most favorite things while she washed and cleaned was listening to the jawing from the rocking chairs and watching the lighting bugs float in the yard with their lazy blinking. In those moments of flight and light, love and family, she believed in the divine.

In September, the bump in her belly starting to show, Papa and Mr. Larsson were planning for a later harvest. With the mild temperatures of Indian Summer lingering there would be plenty of time.

"I can only work at one speed, Papa. We will get done what we can, when we can," Linnea told her father.

Lincoln's horse was for riding, and Custer already had commitments. Linnea's farming efforts were smaller in scale than Papa and Mr. Larsson. She cared for the chickens, her three goats, and the cow. While Mr. Larsson and his boys managed both his land and the adjoining land she owned, Linnea kept her garden filled with the seasonal best, filling the storm cellar with the results of her smoking, pickling, and salting. Her pantry in the kitchen was dry. These were good habits Mama and Papa raised her on. Her endless productivity drew comments from Lincoln. "I have my employment at the asylum. You have your accounting in the city. Why are you busy the rest of the days?"

It wasn't in Linnea's nature to slow down. There was always one more thing to do, something she *could* do before the next day. When challenged she would quote Chaucer, "engage in some occupation, so that the devil may always find you busy." Most did not understand her reply and politely let her be.

In mid October, the wind picked up. Thursday was a beautiful autumn day in Michigan with blue skies, the hint of color in the leaves, the air a little cooler. Friday morning, the sixteenth of October, Lincoln insisted on riding to work because of the increased winds. When he didn't return home that night, she knew he had stayed at his room in the asylum because of the brewing storm. It was frightening to be alone. *What if the new house couldn't stand? What if the second story were to collapse? Was the house too big to stand a big storm?* All night the winds tested the walls of the new home. Expecting and alone she didn't dare step foot outside even though it was tempting to go across the way to be safe with Mama and Papa. Rain and sleet pelted the windows, keeping Linnea from sleep. It was the worst storm she could remember. The rain seemed horizontal cutting across the open lands to her back porch. In the darkness, curled under a blanket for warmth, her mind accounted for the garden in back. What would be the state of things when light broke?

Darkness lingered longer than she expected. The muffled noises of wind allowed her a few moments of rest under a pillow. Opening her eyes to explore what remained from nature's war on her house overnight, she found the windows blocked. She bundled tight as the temperatures had dropped to winter conditions. The windows were darkened from snow. All the windows on the main floor were blocked by large drifts of the white stuff. Attempting to open the door she survived a small avalanche that landed inside. The rest was a thick icy shell.

Upstairs in their master bedroom, she looked out across the white frozen tundra that covered everything. On the west side of the house, the drift went all the way to the second floor window. She could barely make out the fence line marking the road through all the bluster.

Linnea went to the fireplace on the first floor and started a small fire, adding one chunk of coal from the bucket. She wanted to save the rest for later. In the kitchen she lit the wood stove with the minimal kindling not knowing how long the storm would last. With an extra layer of warm clothing and the two fires started, the house started to become a more welcoming place.

In the pantry she opened a jar of preserved cucumber. Cutting it in half, she returned the remainder and lightly salted what she had in hand. It tasted delicious and gave her a bit of vigor to have something in her belly besides the baby.

Linnea was not a fair maiden from a Grimms' tale needing rescue. She had the choice to wait for someone or to do something. Her next thought was for her daily chores. How had the goats, chickens, and cow fared?

With the poker from the fireplace and a kitchen broom Linnea began her work on the back door ice block. It made a mess inside as each chip that landed indoors eventually turned to a puddle. Once she had a hole large enough to escape, she returned to the pantry for the mop and cleaned the puddles. Aglow from work, she thought more about the cucumber. The pang in her stomach called out for more. She took the moment, hot from work, to eat the second half with a little salt.

With broom in hand to steady her balance on the ice, Linnea cautiously advanced across the back porch and down the back steps. The thick snow was past her waist and crusty on top, making it difficult to move. What would normally have been a few floating steps out the back door to the barn took her more than an hour to get a quarter of the way. The broom in her hand burned her skin from the effort of hacking at the crust of ice. If she could get to the barn, she would find the animals and a good shovel for clearing. She needed to reach the barn.

At the halfway mark she was spent. Returning to the house on the carved path was quicker but still took effort. Exhausted, she lay on the kitchen floor, the last of the woodstove's warmth on her face. Everything she had on was drenched from perspiration and melted snow. Feeling alone and sorry for herself, she wasn't sure exactly what to do. She wished that Lincoln would burst through the doors, lift her up like he had when he carried her over the threshold when they first moved into the house and tell her everything would be well. Or for Abell or Papa to make it across the road somehow, that there was something to make it easier for them to dig out a trail and reach her. But help was not on the way. She was her own best hope.

When the moment had passed and with the cold creeping across her skin, she stood back up and added more wood to the fire and stove. She hung her clothing and winter jacket on the back of a chair near the stove to dry and went upstairs to get a fresh outfit. She hated that all of her decisions to this point had filled her wardrobe with dresses. Deeper in her exploration of the wardrobe she found the perfect outfit. A little snug with a baby in waiting, her clothes borrowed from her days in Hillsdale were thick and warm and, most importantly, dry. Her fingertips found that old familiar tingle from the head scarf in her pocket. She thought of R.F. as she always had when she touched the scarf and wondered what had become of his life. She removed the scarf and placed it on her head, tight in the back to hold all of her hair. It felt familiar, yet different without her youthful braided pigtails. Next, she took one of Lincoln's field jackets and put it on like a suit of armor. She could feel the warmth return to her limbs. Lincoln had left his winter gloves and taken his riding gloves. He was likely regretting that today.

Following another whole cucumber, she worked her way

through the icy door hole and the passage made from her morning's labor. The wind cut sharp and cold across her face, the only uncovered part of her above the snowline. With broom and poker she started to chip away at the ice encrusted snow again. She found a rhythm to the effort that seemed to work well without wasting energy, hacking with the poker at the ice, followed by brushing away the snow in larger sweeping motions with the broom. The wind carried the excess snow from her path away.

Three cucumbers and several hours later, she reached the barn door. With each strike of the ice she could hear the hungry animals calling out to her, which gave her hope they were all in good condition. Her heart raced as she broke the ice from the barn door, taking the last of her might as she finally opened it and scurried inside. Light and wind found its way inside through the cracks in the walls. A few deep breaths, a moment's recovery on the hay, and she would stand again. Those few breaths were followed by a few more, and another round. The whole time the goats butted and nuzzled against her jacket, pushing her for food and attention.

"Half a cup of grains each," she said as she put their servings into the feeding trough. "Don't fight. We might have to make this last a week."

The cow chewed its cud and had been grazing on the hay without question. Her oats came in a larger pail. She blinked her big eyes in thanks for the food. Linnea took the stool and pail from the wall to set up near her hind. Would she produce? The cow was on a schedule. She might also be full. Linnea didn't want to break that cycle. With each stroke the milk squirted into the bucket. Once things started to flow, she sang "Green Grow the Lilacs" to keep rhythm and calm the spirits. Wearing her scarf again reminded her of the days when she had longed for R.F. like only a child understands love. She thought of him when she heard this popular song. And she sang, "I once had a sweetheart," squirt-squirt, "but now I have none," squirt-squirt, "the way he had done me," squirt-squirt, "I care for not one." Squirt-squirt, "Since he's gone and left me," squirt-squirt, "contented I'll be," squirt-squirt, "for he loves another," squirt-squirt, "better than me."

She went through the entire song five times before the bucket was full and the cow empty. Lifting the bucket, she took it to the station in the barn she had set up for processing. The milk was poured from the pail by hand over a cloth into a container below, filtering out anything unwanted. The container had a better handle and was easier to carry to the house. When she returned from the house, she rinsed out the pail and returned it and the stool to the peg on the wall above all the animals.

Chickens in their houses were bunched together for warmth. Linnea had set things for the warmer Indian Summer which they enjoyed until that night. With a few minutes of work, fresh bedding was down for extra warmth. She returned to the house with sixteen fresh eggs and one chicken who froze to death that she would pluck and skin.

Still, there was no let up from the storm as the daylight

faded. No word from Lincoln. No word from Papa, Mama, or Abell. Being alone had not bothered her when she had the option of choice. She could decide to stay or go. But the forced isolation reminded her of so many bad times. The time at the textile when they thought she was sick. Alone in a hotel room. Alone on the train. Left with strangers. Her stories from that time had gone unspoken. She never trusted herself to tell Mama, Papa, or Abell everything. While she loved Lincoln with all her heart, he didn't know she had been to Detroit. Every opportunity had passed without saying a word. She would never tell. All those adventures and feelings, all the actions, seem like a lifetime ago. As if they had happened to another person.

In some ways she guessed that they had. She was a different Linnea now. These things were so far in the past, they would never catch up to now. While she poured the milk into separate containers of wax seal jars, she thought about the boy. It had been a long while since she allowed herself to think of him. Loneliness and giving up the boy were two dark spots without any hope of light. It never felt right to leave the boy. Head over heart, she knew he would have a better life, but that knowledge never made it hurt less. "Canterbury Tales," she thought to herself, "engage in some occupation, so that the devil may always find you busy." With the remaining milk poured into the churn, Linnea started to work the handle and pump. The pumping action was best done to a rhythm and step, and she started to sing, "When

Johnny comes marching home again, hurrah, hurrah. We'll give him a hearty welcome then, hurrah, hurrah."

Howls from the wind could not keep her up that night. She was exhausted. She had not felt this tired since her first week at the textile mill. As an adult, it didn't bother her. It was merely work.

By the long day's end, Linnea had a clear path to the barn and warm and fed animals. There were two jars of steamed milk in the pantry, and a fresh pound of butter. After cooking something for herself, there were a dozen eggs remaining and sure to be more on the way. There is always something to do on a farm, always a way to keep the body busy and the mind clear. And always better days ahead.

CHAPTER 29

The wind never stopped. It was angry, cold, and constantly blowing. Stretches throughout the night surged in intensity. Like the Big Bad Wolf, it huffed and puffed at the doors, rattled the windows, and found every uncovered space trying to get in. Under all the blankets Linnea laid in bed until first light. She was sore from the previous day's work. She felt feeble as she attempted to lift the blankets. Papa had told her stories from Sweden, growing up in the sod house with bitter winters. She had never known them to be this bad, but imagined this must have been what it was like in the old country. This storm had come on quickly and brought so much snow for this early in the year. But she was confident that it might last only another day or two before moving on, and there would be the mud to deal with before they could harvest. *How much of*

the harvest can we save? Have I stored enough in the cellar? When will Lincoln come home?

Sweeping through the overnight drifts back into the barn, she completed her chores nearly normally. Rather than full feed portions for the animals she kept, she decided that until the break in weather, she would serve about seventy-five percent to stretch things. Even if the storm was to last a few days, it might be longer before getting more feed and grain. The road would certainly be muddy ruts, slowing down buggies and buckboards. Linnea kept a good face in front of the goats and cow, singing to them as she worked. The chickens greeted her in a flurry of activity, happy to be relieved of the extra eggs and grateful to fill their bellies.

The metal spade for the garden seemed the perfect tool for her plan. She carried it through the house to the front door and began to chip away at the winter wall. Once she broke through the thick ice shell, she expanded the hole and closed the door behind her. Her new wrap-around porch held mounds of wind-blown snow, making it creak under the strain of her footsteps. Again, she found the right rhythm to scoop and throw it over the railing into the yard. Each time took a great deal of strength as she needed to clear over the drifts and make headway against the wind. Reaching the steps, she took a break, carrying the spade inside with her.

The few embers in the fireplace helped to start another log and chunk of coal and keep the interiors acceptable. In the kitchen stove, she added a few more pieces of split wood to keep everything from freezing. Today's menu included two eggs and a thick slice of bread. There was more than enough for two this week, but she had to also keep things from spoiling and going to waste. It was an odd balance to find in rationing: try not to waste, but do not eat too much to save some for later.

Rested and wrapped for the polar conditions, she ventured back to the front porch steps. Spade in hand and revitalized for the next round, she thrust the warm metal tip against the rocky ice to clear away the wintry remains. Click-tick-tick, the tip cut into the frozen water. Shup-shup, the snow was thrown into the front yard. Click-tick-tick, she continued to chip away. Choosh-choosh, the spade scraped before throwing snow over the drift.

At the bottom of the stairs Linnea took a moment to review her work. Now that the steps were entirely clear of snow with one safety rail free should Abell come to visit, she felt accomplished. Turning to make a path to the Papa and Mama's, she found the snow in front of her was now waist high. The drifts had been building the entire time and partially protecting her while she worked on the porch. Her problem had been growing by several inches the entire time.

She took hold of the spade and felt the hours of work tingle in her hand. She was sure to have blisters to lance that night. Her forward thrust of the metal spade was stopped in its advance. The expected sound was replaced by a twang of metal and a sharp crack. On close inspection the metal had split vertically in two to the wooden handle. Testing it on another scoop of snow, it lifted a smaller than normal amount. In her thrust to throw the snow over the drift, the metal head went flying into the yard with the snow. She was left with only a handle and heartache.

She took refuge inside by the fire under all the blankets. Her clothes hung to dry nearby. A new strategy needed to form. Linnea would not be able to retrieve the spade head until the snow melted. She could not see any success of trying to climb over the snowdrifts as they were now nearly as high as her shoulder. It would take all her care to keep the path in the back passable. There was a shovel in the barn, but its head was flat for scooping. Her goal was no longer to clear the snow, but make it something to walk on.

Warmed, fed, and in a dry outfit, with kitchen broom and fireplace scoop in hand she cleared the path to the barn again. Her flat shovel was where she expected. She also took the hand saw this time.

With the hand saw she made her way to the beech tree. It took the better part of an hour to get the ten yards, and another hour to cut the five-year-old tree down. It was roughly ten feet tall with several branches, making it ideal for her needs. She cut the branches and plucked the leaves. Finally, she dragged the whole thing into the house where she sat by the fire for several hours weaving her plan into existence.

The next morning, waking under all the blankets at first light, she was excited to try her new creation. Bundled tight to face the constant winds, the spade handle in one hand and the shovel in the other, she secured the hand-made snowshoes on her feet to venture out the front door again. The beech bark was perfect for making a taunt wrapping to hold the elastic branches and trunk in place. She had shaped her creation into a "bear paw" design that should keep her above the deep snows. With her shovel, she cleared the porch again. As she looked down the steps, she should remove the snowshoes and walk to the bottom and put them back on. This was her first trial, and she had to allow for mistakes. Tender footed, her first step on the snow took half her weight. Leaning fully she stayed on top of the frozen landscape. With her right foot now pressing down, she thought to herself, *"walking on water, the easiest of miracles."*

Walking to Papa and Mama's house would normally take less than five minutes from door to door. Under the gray and snowy skies, wind pressing against her, and each step under caution, it took her a full hour on her first attempt.

"Oh, my baby!" Mama cried, hugging her at the door. "We were worried about you."

Papa patted Linnea on the back. "That's my true American, making a way against everything."

Mama peppered Linnea with questions about supplies necessary to ensure her daughter's safety, to which Linnea answered, "Yes, Mama, I have that," each time. More than anything she needed the company of others. It had been three days since she saw another human, and that was too long for her.

"Sure, sure, we saw big snow back home, but nothing like this. It went from autumn to blizzard overnight. We might see half this snow in the old country, but it would take a month, not a day."

"And the sod house was warmer," Mama added. "We were basically living underground. It kept things much warmer."

No one had heard or seen Abell and Anna. "Well, we didn't want to bother your brother. We thought they would come in if they got hungry or cold."

Linnea knocked before trying the door of the barn. The journey took her several minutes to get across the yard, but she thought it important to check in.

"Come in," Abell said.

"Abell? How are you? How are you making out here?"

"Fine, fine" He was brushing Custer as if it were another day.

"We were worried about you."

"Why?"

"Well, the weather. We didn't see you."

"We are fine in here."

"Is Anna Olsen with you?"

"Yes, Linna. I'm well, thank you," Anna said from the hay loft. "Getting some more hay for Custer."

The barn felt cozy and warm, protecting them from the outside world. "You have enough to eat?"

"We are fine, Linnea. The hens are still laying, and Custer has enough oats. We are keeping the stove running so the water hand pump won't freeze."

Linnea's face went white. She had never considered the

water pipe for indoor plumbing. Would that freeze? What would happen if it did?

"I should go. Glad to hear you are all well." Linnnea turned to head back out the door.

"Linnea, what are those on your feet?"

"Snowshoes, made from the beech tree that was in our backyard.

"Huh, that's pretty smart, little sister," he laughed. "Come back later. Show Anna how you made them, and I'll have her make three,"

The return trip to her house was much faster now that there was a packed trail. Her familiar steps tracked across the yard to the road and up a steep bank to her front yard. There were fresh steps, much deeper, next to her path. Looking up and through the blowing snow she made out the light from her front window. Someone had let himself in. Was it Lincoln? Had he made it all this way back to her? Or someone else in desperation?

CHAPTER 30

"*H*iram?"

The lurking figure stood by the fire. At his feet, bundled under all the blankets, lay "Lucky Lincoln."

"I found him in a drift 'bout a mile back."

"What were you doing out?"

Hiram looked down at Lincoln, "He will need to warm for a while. He was half frozen when I found him. Check for frostbite."

"Thank you, Hiram. Thank you for bringing him back to me. Can I fix you something to eat? You must be starving to make your way through this."

There was only a grunt and the slightest of nods from the poorly lit face in the dark room.

"I am going to warm water, and make eggs. We have

181

plenty, and can't let it spoil. You sit by the fire and make yourself comfortable."

She took the big metal tub for washing and set it in the kitchen, making several trips to the back door to fill the pots with snow, melting it over the fire and pouring it into the wash tub. At the same time she fried eggs and bread in the iron pan, enough for ten men.

"Help me get him to the kitchen, Hiram." She could tell he was resistant to the light in the kitchen. "Please help."

The two carried Lincoln from the floor in the front room to the kitchen table where they propped him up in a chair, shoes tenderly removed, and feet without socks placed in the warm tub. Hiram added a few blankets over his shoulder as Lincoln hunched over the tub. The teepee of blankets captured all the moist warmth and started to thaw him.

"Figured he had been trying to get here, out in the elements at least two days by looks."

"Thank you for bringing him here. You never said what you were doing all this way out."

Hiram cleared his throat and said, "Well, I would be lying if I told you anything other than checking on you."

His words came as a surprise, and she whispered, "All those years, I stayed away."

"You stayed at a distance," he nodded knowingly. "You didn't stay away. And I appreciate that."

There was no fooling Hiram. When Linnea sat and watched from the hotel porch drinking her tea conveniently at the same time his train passed through for years, word eventually got to him. While the blow to his head may have slowed him down over the years, he was no goose.

"You look well."

"Thank you."

"Have you been well?"

"We were on our run from Saginaw to Detroit when the storm hit about ten miles north of Pontiac. Those last miles were slow. We fought for every inch thinking the winds might push us off the tracks. We've been stopped at Pontiac station since. The engine went cold. It'll take a day or more to clear her and start up again. Even the telegraph wires are down. No getting word out to anyone, not like they could do something anyway."

"I asked how you were."

He thought on it before answering, "It's good to see you again. I'm happy for that."

Linnea smiled, and felt a natural blush, "It's good to see you too, Hiram." He still had a way about him.

"I recognized Lincoln from the paper announcing his position at the asylum. The initials on his case matched. Not many L.B.'s in these parts. Happy for you, good you could meet someone. Good to know you aren't alone. He takes good care of you?"

"He does." She took three of the eggs from the skillet with the fried bread and flipped them on a plate. She handed him the plate with a fork.

Hiram took the plate and fork, sat at the far end of the

kitchen table, facing her, watching Lincoln melt from his statue-like state.

"Salt and pepper." She set the shakers on the table within Hiram's reach. "The coffee isn't hot, but it will taste good." She poured him a warm cup and set it next to the salt and pepper.

When the smell of eggs reached him under the blanket tent and the sound of sizzling eggs popped enough, Lincoln moaned, "My feet."

She helped him get his head out from under the layers. Her smile was the first thing he saw upon thawing back to life. "Linnea?"

"You're home." She stood next to him and rubbed his shoulders vigorously.

"Thank God, I made it. Last I remember was a bear following me."

"Did the bear look like that?" Linnea pointed to Hiram.

"Oh, yes. It did…"

"That's Hiram, the postman from the train. He found you in a snow drift."

"Hiram, I owe you my life. Thank you."

"You're welcome, Lucky Lincoln."

"Oh, you don't know how lucky I am." Lincoln looked to Linnea.

"Last I hear, they're calling it the 'Alpena Storm.' It sent a flat boat out of Chicago to the bottom of Lake Michigan. Wind's so bad, it flipped that flat boat. Can you imagine?"

"I think I can. Those winds nearly took the roof off," Linnea replied.

"How's Mama and Papa?" Lincoln asked.

"They are doing fine. Those two old Swedes thought nothing of the storm, and Abell and Anna are waiting things out in the barn with Custer." She put the back of her hand on Lincoln's forehead, smiled, and fixed his hair with her fingers. "You, you need some rest. Why didn't you stay? You didn't have to come home."

"Needed to make sure you were safe."

Looking in his eyes, Linnea could feel that pang in her heart at the thought of losing Lincoln. There had been many years, she had to face so much alone, she couldn't imagine what she would do now without him.

"How is the baby?" he asked.

"We're fine, just fine." She smiled.

With a creak in the chair from Hairm's shift in weight, Linnea realized that the show of affection between her and her husband made him uncomfortable. She withdrew her hand from Lincoln's hair and pulled the blanket tight around his shoulders. "Hiram, would you like more eggs? I have more on the stove."

"No, thank you, Mrs. Beaumont. I appreciate you feeding me, but I should make my way back to the train."

Hearing Hiram say her formal name "Mrs. Beaumont" took her by surprise. It sounded foreign to hear him say it. She had always liked the way he said Linnea. "Really? On a night like this? Won't you stay, keep warm till it passes?"

"Mrs. Beaumont, this storm may be here a while, and I can't afford to stay overnight if they get the train running. I am, after all, the postmaster for this line."

"Postmaster? What a fine title you've earned. Good for you, Hiram. Good for you!"

She walked him to the front door, broom in hand in case it was needed, and tugged on his coat a bit to make certain it was tight as could be. "Do you need gloves? A hat?"

"Thank you, Mrs. Beaumont. I have what I need."

"Please, stop with the 'Mrs. Beaumont'. You can call me Linnea."

"Mrs. Beaumont, that ain't right. Thank you for the meal."

"Thank you for saving my husband."

"For that, you are welcome."

CHAPTER 31

$\mathcal{I}$t took a week before the hard winds softened. During that time Linnea and Lincoln had memorized the paper from the week prior. It became a little joke between the two of them, walking through the house and quoting the most random topics time and again.

"Did you know there is a Gymnastics Exhibition at the dance hall Friday night?"

"Dawsons Superior Flour has a new process!"

"Dear, did you know that Grand Rapids Plaster is only $4.50 a ton at the Lord Elevator? It's the highly celebrated Kelly Island Lime."

"McConnell's CARPETS! CARPETS! CARPETS!"

Linnea put on her snowshoes and visited Abell in the barn once he returned from taking Anna home and Lincoln to the asylum.

"How was the trip?"

"Custer moved at a fast clip in the snow. His breath in winter looked like the steam from a locomotive engine when he got going. Those open country miles were straight and fast."

"What's it like in the city?"

"Only a single path in each direction on the streets, twenty foot mountains of snow drifts on each side. It was unlike anything I've ever seen."

"And the Olsens."

Abell gave a grimaced glare while brushing Custer. "The first stop was the Olson farm. I could hear the questions from her parents they hadn't asked in front of me as we pulled away."

"I am sure they'll understand. The two of you would have surely died if you tried to bring her home before it was safe. Look what happened with Lincoln."

"I know for a fact, even if there was a question, that Anna remained true and pure. To make good and restore the faith, I have decided to ask for her hand in marriage, if she will have me."

"That would be wonderful. It will be nice to finally have a sister. I am very happy for you. She will say yes."

"Do you think?"

"I do. You would be a great husband for Anna."

Abell, like nearly every Swede she had ever known, was reserved with their emotions. So he changed the conversation topic to something other than the matters of the heart. "Twenty-foot snow drifts along the street, with cuts at the entry of each store from the road. There must have been a hundred men with shovels marching like the union army to the train station, all hired to dig a path to Detroit."

"That many men in the city?"

"Everything slowed to a snail's pace, I saw a dozen people slip and fall. A blast of wind swept through the town and carried a man twenty feet before he could stand up. Telegraph poles snapped in two, wires were on the ground, the city was a mess. Count yourself lucky the new house was complete and built to stand the winter."

"Oh, I do! It sounds like an adventure, Abell. Thank you for getting Lincoln to work. Did he say when he might be back? How long might he stay?"

"Depends on the weather, I suppose. The asylum is full up. My guess is he will be there a month if the weather breaks in our favor."

"Oh."

"Baby isn't due for months, right?"

"That's right."

"You have your family right across the way, Linnea. You are going to be fine. Mama has gone through this plenty of times. You shouldn't worry yourself. First time with Mama here, you will be fine."

She heard the words "first time" and was reminded that only four people knew her secret. She wasn't able to tell her family, friends, and most certainly not her husband. Not five years ago the Sjolander girl four farms over was rumored to be with child outside of marriage, and a week later the family was gone. No farwell, no good-bye, or explanation. They lifted up everything and "moved west" is what everyone said. Linnea couldn't tell Abell. Never a word to Lincoln. "Oh, I'm not worried about that. I hate that Lincoln's not here."

"You must love him."

"I do, I really do."

"May I confide in you, my dear sister?"

"I wish you would."

"I don't want to be a burden."

"Never."

"I saw you and Lincoln, the better part of a few years apart in age, and how you two are happy together. Things work between you in ways, well, in ways I didn't know possible. And I saw you at the wedding, happy. It's been a long time alone since the war. I've never felt whole, always missing something, more than my leg and arm. But when I saw you and Lincoln, I knew that I could allow myself to love."

"That might be the sweetest thing I've heard."

"It's no secret I am a broken man. Anna see's past that. Together, things fit, they work. I never knew I could love like that until you and Lincoln showed me."

"Abell, you have to ask for her hand. The years between

you don't matter. I've read of greater distances in age between southern generals and girls who've set aside their dolls for an old man and a pension. And you, my dear older brother, are not *that* old, and Anna must love you."

Abell smiled in Linnea's delight to tease him. "Speaking of reading, I've got the latest paper for you." He removed it from his side satchel. "Lots for you to catch up on."

"Thank you very much. I was growing tired of the paper from two weeks ago and needed something new to read. Oh, look, Dawsons Superior Four has a new process." Her smile grew thinking of the week she and Lincoln had had to themselves.

"Is that good news?"

"It is for me."

"With the corn still in the field, and potatoes frozen, I am sure there is a lot of rot on the way. This harvest is going to be poor. That new process might mean more than you know for wheat and flour."

"Yes, dear brother. I am happy to have a cow and goats with a good amount of grain for the month. I have to keep those rats from the barn and everything will be fine."

She could have stayed the night. She could have walked across the yard and crawled into the loft onto her mattress to be with Mama and Papa. Instead, she made her way back to the empty house across the road.

Once inside, with the door closed, she could hear the wind pick up where it had left off the day before last. The howl as it passed the house, the rattles when it teased the windows, and the drafts when it found every crack in the seams. With a few more flakes starting in the sky, Linnea knew that Lincoln might be gone longer than a month. The three empty bedrooms felt the size of the Taj Mahal without anyone in them. *What more could I do today?* She asked herself.

CHAPTER 32

On the next passable day from winter's constant presence, Linnea took the last of her coins and convinced Abell to take her to town. The destination was McConnell's, and they were there for CARPETS! CARPETS! CARPETS! They were also finishing the house with drapes. She planned to put carpets in the main room and hang drapes on all of the first floor windows and some of the outside walls. These fabrics would help to insulate the house from the early winter.

"I've never seen someone inspect fabric like that before," Abell said as he watched Linnea finger a blue gingham. .

"If you spent a year at the textile, you would know the differences. McConnell's would take the less savvy shopper for a run."

The project was an excellent use of indoor time for Abell and Linnea. In Papa's barn they worked to make the modelings and stain the woods with beeswax. Abell could work wonders in metal as he hammered away with his one good hand. "Imagine if I still had them both!" he joked once. But the one was more than good enough for what Linnea needed. From the top of an apple box, she could hang the drapes to frame the window. From the same perch the entry was shrouded from the winds. At the end of the three-day project, winter was still an early and unexpected guest, but they felt the accomplishment of a job well done to plan for winter's stay.

"Why don't you stay here, Abell?" Linnea asked. "One less trip across the road. I will make you supper. You can stay nice and toasty here with me."

"I would like that," Abell said. "But I promised Mama to help her tonight with a similar project."

"Oh." She did her best not to look crestfallen. "We want Papa and Mama to be warm this winter. Thank you for agreeing to help them."

A NEW SOUND in the night woke Linnea. She had gotten accustomed to the whoosh of the winds and rattles of windows. This new sound was a scratch at the back door. It was a soft pawing sound that grew with intensity. By lamp light, she braced herself for a cold blast, and opened the door. The desperate black eyes looked up from the orange fur at her feet. It was skittish at first, not sure whether to stay or run into the cold night. This American Red Fox was brave enough to scratch the back door for help.

Linnea found a tug of smoked meat in one of the wax seal jars and dropped it to the fox on the porch. Quickly the pointed nose found it and took it twenty steps away to devour it.

"You must not be able to get in the hen house, Mr. Fox." Before she could close the door, the fox returned to the porch. With a crack of the door open, it's little nose sniffed inside.

"Are you coming in? Or staying out. The door is going to close. Make a decision."

With that said, the fox lowered to nearly a crawl, dragging its lean belly across her kitchen floor. Its eyes followed Linnea the entire time, wondering in wait, ready to spring away if threatened. Linnea closed the door tight and pulled the thick tapestry along the rail and hook to keep drafts away.

In the kitchen's corner were remnants left from her curtain project. Mr. Fox snuck to the pile and walked atop it in circles, until it decided it was right. In a quick moment, the fox was in a ball laying on top, tail tucked under its nose, eyes watching Linnea's next move.

Certain her new friend would make a mess, she took the

oldest newspaper and lay it out around the new bed it had claimed. At the edge, she placed a bowl with water, and another tug of smoked meat.

"You aren't my first fox," she said. "I knew a man named Rhett Fox Slater almost two decades ago. He was also a charmer that snuck into my life."

The fox simply blinked at her from its perch, seeming less threatened at being this close.

"Would you prefer Mr. Fox? Or do you want to be called R.F.?"

She heard a slight whimper from the animal.

"Mr. Fox it is. R.F. would only make me feel more alone."

Linnea placed a few more logs from the fire box into the kitchen stove. It kept the room warm to let it burn all day, and with the doorway to the front room unblocked, much of the work of heating was shared between the stove and fireplace. The new fabric covers between entrances boxed the heat in to make it toasty by the fireplace. Instead of going to the bedroom, she slept by the fire for the night.

Before daybreak, the eerie howl of Mr. Fox caused her to leap from the high back chair. Mr. Fox, sitting in front of the fireplace, watching her sleep, was now tired of her company and compassion. Mr. Fox demanded to go outside and face the winter.

Heart racing from the ghostly morning call, she pulled back the door's curtain, and opened it enough to let him out. His nose made it outside, and he sniffed. Feeling the bitter wind on its front, and warmth on its back, Mr. Fox looked up to Linnea with a moment's doubt before dashing out, leaping off the back porch, and disappearing into the deep snows. It bounded up and over the snowline, time and again making great leaps until it was gone into the darkness.

CHAPTER 33

*B*y American Thanksgiving, Lincoln had been home a total of two days. The early winter had become a long winter. Abell was correct in his prediction: there was nothing but rot in the fields, and no harvest. No harvest meant no money. For many, no money meant unpaid debts for seed, supplies, and equipment. There wasn't much to be thankful for that season but each other. Even that was in short supply for Linnea.

Each morning the trail made the day prior was windswept and often deeper with drifting snow than the day before. Abell told her that the one hundred men shoveling snow for the rail line had grown in size to over five hundred. If you had a strong back it meant a steady pay.

"Joe Wilson," Abell said, "was found frozen in a drift not two days ago. They think he was walking the tracks at night and the conductor didn't see him. The walls of the snow cut were at least fifteen feet, taller than the train. Old Joe had nowhere to go. Couldn't get out of the way of the engine. It must have hit him hard and threw him over the cut and out of the way."

Linnea covered her mouth and shook her head. "How awful!"

"It is awful."

"What else is going on in the city? I miss going there daily. Your reports are welcome as the paper grows stale."

"Well, you know about the snow storm, right?"

The two laughed.

"The icehouse is cutting blocks early on the lake and river this year. They can't seem to find enough men to work for them. I guess the normal crew are shoveling snow. Shoveling snow pays better these days, I hear."

"I see."

"And there was word that scarlet fever is on the decline. Fewer people see each other it seems."

"Oh, interesting."

"Do you know the postmaster by chance?"

"Hiram? Why, yes, I do." Linnea's interest bloomed. "Why do you ask?"

"Well, I saw him on my trip to town, and he asked how you were. It caught me, as I had never heard him talk before, and then to have him ask about you."

"Well, I know many people, Abell. I am well known in this city. It should not surprise you."

"I didn't mean to ruffle your feathers. I had no idea you two knew one another."

Linnea had a choice in truths to share with Abel. One that took place twenty years ago, and the other which happened last month. *Both were honest*, she convinced herself. *I'm not lying to Abel.*

"He saved Lincoln from freezing to death in a snowbank last month. Hiram was the one who found him and brought him home. There is no mystery to solve. We know each other, that's all. Saved my husband from certain death."

Abell reached into his satchel and removed the most recent paper along with letters. "He gave me these for you, and the paper is from me."

"Thank you very much, Abell. You are the best big brother a girl could ask for."

Abell stood in his slow and unique manner of hopping and leaning onto the cane which had become part of his identity.

"Abell, how much firewood remains for Mama and Papa?"

"Do you need wood?"

"Well, it's not running out, but we are using it sparingly."

"I can spare a few, I mean, if you need it."

"It's not that. I was wondering, as the winter goes on, if it doesn't make sense for you, Papa and Mama to come live here."

"Live here?"

"Yes, well, there is plenty of room. We could combine our

efforts under one roof. It's not like the census taker is coming back again this year. It's just..."

"I will see what the other two say. Your proposal makes a good deal of sense to me."

"Abell, why do you risk frequenting the city? It seems awfully dangerous for you, for Custer. What could be that important?"

Abell chuckled, "It's my excuse to see Anna. I'm not in the city that long, but happen to pay a visit to her regularly."

"How is her family faring?"

"The Olsens are feeling the pressure of debt collectors. The damned winter has put them at risk, kept them out of the fields. There are only small patches of the land they've been able to work. You asked about firewood, and be certain, you are not alone. There are criminals and thieves stealing kindling and wood from boxes and stores. Honesty is in short supply these days."

"I didn't realize it was getting that bad."

"Well, we're in this together, my dear sister. I think it will be easy to persuade our parents to 'come take care of you here.' It is a new warmer house after all. It's ready for the baby."

IN TWO WEEKS time and after several trips across the road, Papa and Mama had brought everything they needed to Linneas home. Mama insisted on keeping busy in the kitchen, and Linnea had noticed some items moved around. At times it was hard for her to find what she needed. Linnea knew her mother was not moving things out of spite, but Mama struggled to find balance in remembering whose kitchen it was. Papa found the high back chairs a wonder of warmth near the fire. Often he was found "resting his eyes" in one. Custer found a new home in the barn with the cow and goats. All of the chickens were now living in the one hen house at Linnea's home. It made for one big happy family. Reflecting on the last few weeks, Linnea wasn't disappointed to skip American Thanksgiving that year. Being with her family again was what she was truly thankful for.

DURING HIS NEXT VISIT HOME, Lincoln found many changes. His wife was showing and her family was comfortable in his home. He had missed Linnea. He hated that they were separated. He told her how he longed to be with her and tried to find those private moments to share alone in their room.

"We should attend the New Years Eve event," he said.

"This New Year? I would love to get out of the house, be together. It sounds lovely, but..."

"But what?"

"Well, I would need a dress, and I am sure at this size, none will fit."

He kissed her sweetly. "You are magical in ways I've never understood, and one of the best with a sewing kit. I am sure you will think of something. How did you become such a talented seamstress? Where did you learn it? Not from your mother, I assume."

"A girl has her secrets, dear husband."

"I can't wait to take you in my arms across the floor, in front of everyone to show off how beautiful you are." He kissed her again and passions began to rise.

"I suppose…" Her mind started to consider her wardrobe. The kisses he lay on her lips and working down to her neck and lower went unnoticed. In her mind's eye the inventory of what she had and what was needed to be at this public event continued until a special tickle sent a tingle through her body causing her to gasp for air. "Oh, Mr. Beaumont!"

THE DANCE HALL was a wonderful and rare heat. It was a pleasure after months of cold to feel the swelter of summer captured in one room. They had had enough of these dark cold rooms isolated from the world. This night had light. The night was warm. The room was filled with beautiful people in beautiful attire. Linnea, fond of her wonderful husband, kissed him on the cheek in public for bringing her.

His reply, in sweet and soft words, "Gymnastics Exhibition at the dance hall Friday night," broke the two into laughter and pure joy.

In an hour, Linnea was aglow in the evenings wonderment. Between the moments of breathlessness from her condition, she desired to be physically closer to her "Lucky Lincoln" but the growing size of her belly kept them apart. "A little champagne won't hurt," she was told, taking a chair and enjoying the view. Several of the families close to her represented the Swedes. She forgot how big and brawny some of the lads were, how elegant the ladies looked. On normal occasions, more times than not they were wearing things caked with mud or well worn from work. Tonight, however, people glittered like never before. Linnea talked to friends as if they had been a lifetime apart. Time-and-again she was told how lovely she looked, how blessed she was to expand the family, and that children are the greatest gift. For years to come, Linnea would look back on this night and remember the moments clearly, as times like this in life are rare and precious.

During the sleigh ride home Custer took Linnea and Lincoln under a clear moonlit night through the calmest weather in months. Every star seemed more brilliant than she could remember, her arm under Lincoln's tight as he clicked and called direction.

"Thank you, Lincoln. I could never have asked for a better night than this. You've been good to me. I love you more than my words can express."

"I love you, Linnea. I am the luckiest man in the world to have you as my wife. I've never known such happiness. It's always felt as if something was missing in my life until I met you, on that street, working on that crew. It's as if we were meant to be. We were meant to be together."

CHAPTER 34

The pantry was noticeably short on supplies by the first week in February. Many trips were made to the cellar where things kept longer to move them to the upstairs pantry. Each time the trip was made, Linnea broke away the ice covering the doors before venturing down. Her sway as she stepped was becoming more of a duck's waddle to take care on the ice and move with the expected baby.

At last, there were no more treacherous trips left. She could count the remaining days they would have food like an advent calendar. But for her, every wax sealed jar and case was more than a treat. It was life. Abell took the goats into town where they were sold to the rail line to feed the army of snow shovelers. The family was down to three chickens who produced eggs still. The rest had been cooked in a pot.

With little oats on ration the cow looked lean and Linnea received less and less milk.

"The cow might need to feed those shovelers," she thought out loud.

"She's not feeding us much longer," Mama said.

Linnea sighed. "I can sell her to the rail line and buy supplies. Or I could take her to the butcher. We would eat well."

"Prices are running out of control," Papa said, "even if you have the money, it won't go nearly as far. Abell, when is that train supposed to come from Detroit?"

"Three weeks ago."

"Best I take her to the butcher for ourselves then. Can't count on supplies to be there."

"Don't know if I trust the butcher," Abell said. "I hear tell he takes more for himself with each cut."

"Well, I can't do it. And you can't do it. Put together the four of us couldn't. I say we take the loss and walk her into town the next day the snow stops."

"Yes, Linnea, you and I can walk her into town after you get the last of her milk. Maybe we can use the last of the oats this week to fatten her up a bit?"

Linnea nodded.

CHAPTER 35

The first pang inside came on April 27, 1881. Linnea had counted only fifteen days when the sun had come out since that October 16 storm. Her family, who the day prior was too tired and sleepy to do more than sit and look at one another, now hovered over her in bed. Their skin white as ghosts, bodies lean like skeletons, each had continued insisting Linnea eat normal portions while they took less.

She knew what that pain meant. It was powerful, but it lacked the impact and surprise from that first time in Hillsdale. Her spoiled sheets twisted under her contortions. Mama encouraged her, coached her, and instructed the boys to boil the snow into water. Everyone did what Mama told them. Linnea pushed, and the men went downstairs.

"Have we gotten word from Lincoln?"

"Not yet, you focus on the baby. Don't worry about Lincoln."

"I want him to be here, Mama. Where is he? Why isn't he here?"

"He will be here soon enough. Don't you worry. Women have been doing this since Eve gave birth to Cain. You are doing fine."

Another spasm inside and Linnea pushed to help the baby along. With the push, Mama exclaimed, "Oh, my!"

"What? What is it?"

The cries of the baby broke the moment of silence

"I didn't expect it to be so fast," Mama said.

Linnea remembered the hours she spent in this condition before. This had been fast. "Is it here?"

"He's here. You have a boy!"

Mama wrapped the child and handed him to his mother.

"Oh, he's beautiful. Mama, don't you think?"

"All babies are beautiful," Mama said.

Papa was first through the door. "Did it happen?"

"He's here. Papa, you are now a Farfar."

Papa looked to see his precious daughter and grandson together. Many babies were small, but his grandson seemed smaller. Still, the pride in his chest grew to see the boy in his mother's arms. "Another true American in the family."

"Congratulations, Linnea," Abell said. "How do you feel?"

"Good. Tired, but good."

"That's normal. Normal for the baby, normal for the mama."

"I'm a mama, Mama!"

"You are, my dear. You certainly are."

The slam of the door downstairs pulled everyone's attention as the patter of fast footfalls ran up the stairs. "Linnea? Linnea?"

"In here."

Lincoln came through the bedroom door. "He's here? I missed it?"

"You didn't miss anything. Your timing is impeccable, Lucky Lincoln. He arrived just before you came through the door."

"Congratulations, Lincoln. It's a boy."

"A boy! Oh, let me see." Lincoln kneeled at the bedside to be near his wife and child. "Oh honey, a boy." Lincoln poked at the sheets to get a better look. "Is he, I mean, is everything well?"

"He's a normal baby, Lincoln," Mama said. "You're a proud papa."

"Most babies are small," Papa added.

"What do I know?" He chuckled nervously. "It's my first. All I care about is that my beautiful wife and boy are healthy. That's what makes me happy."

"What's his name?" Abell asked.

Lincoln looked at Linnea, "What do you think?"

"William. His name is William."

"I like that name. William it is. I will wire my parents. They are sure to come to meet their grandson when the weather breaks."

"I look forward to finally meeting them."

"They are going to love you, Linnea. I know they will." He kissed her forehead and began to stroke her hair.

"Abell, why don't you and I get some wood to burn. William will need a warm home."

"Papa, what happened to your house while I was gone?" Lincoln asked.

"We've been using it in the fireplace." Abell answered.

"Sure, sure, it's good dry wood. Burns fast. So we started to take the place apart to warm this place."

"The trees are green wood, frozen, even when we cut it down and dry it in the barn, it takes weeks to get it dry enough for the fire."

"Things are that tough? Makes sense."

"Things are tough here. Lincoln. Looks like they feed you well at the asylum." Abell joked.

Good hearted Lincoln laughed at the honest jab. "It's true, we haven't skipped a meal."

"You two enjoy the moment, we've got wood to gather," Papa said on his way out of the room.

"Mama," Lincoln asked, "is William small for a baby? He seems small."

"All my boys were big, big boys. Some babies are small. William is still good and healthy. Don't you worry."

CHAPTER 36

ay was the month of mud. The longest winter had finally ended, its snow had begun to melt, turning the world into thick, gooey mud that caked on every foot, hoof, and paw. To stand still was to risk sinking into its sticky suction. The snow had been bad. The mud, worse. Mud Lake earned its name at the back of Papa's property, water levels rising with the melt, covering more than half the land. The wood pile created from the old house had sunk into an irretrievable muck.

Roads to town became impassable on the third day after the wheels were put back on the buckboard. Word that the rail company didn't trust the tracks to hold brought the whole system to a halt. No shoveler could clear this path. No blade on the locomotive could find a way.

The river was up. It crested above the axle of the water

wheel, flooding the ground floor of the mill. Anything they still had in reserve in the stores was now washed downstream along with the porch at the Summit and the whole of the Hotel Clinton.

William had been in the world of cold and mud for a month by the time life in Pontiac returned to something close to normal. Ruts in the road were obstacles Custer enjoyed going around. The earth began to harden, but missed most of the topsoil. One of the first trains from Detroit brought relief from Toledo and the Ohio farms now producing on the drained Great Black Swamp. Fuel, food, fresh waster, and equipment were delivered in one of the best days the city could remember. Linnea and Lincoln could see the turn for the future improve as the train unloaded.

Telegraph lines returned to operation which allowed Lincoln to write his parents with the good news. He invited them to visit during the month of June, after the school term ended for his father's teaching.

Abell and Anna made plans for a July wedding after gaining permission from her father. It was the perfect time of year for the public celebration of their love. It fell between planting and harvest. This year's soil would be ready. The two families could come together closer as one, no longer only good friends in the community. The Olsens and Karlssons would now be the biggest family in size and respect among the Swedes.

"My true American," Papa said to Linnea, "we are all

joining you at the train station to meet the Beaumonts. We will be one big, happy family."

"I am nervous, Papa. I don't know what they will think of me. Lincoln hardly says a word about them. Even when he does, it's only a little and not much in detail. What if they think I'm not a monster?"

"Sure, sure, it's normal to be a little nervous. How could they think you a monster? You are beautiful. You give them a grandson. You take care of their son. Most importantly, he loves you. And if they don't, Mama and I will make up for it."

His encouraging words brought a smile to her face. These words kept her strong in the days leading to her in-laws' arrival. She took comfort knowing she would always have Mama and Papa, they would always be there to love her.

WILLIAM, in his best pink outfit, stayed close to his mother in the coach the entire trip. With his nestle and coo, his kicking legs, he was the perfect baby who slept through the night and rarely fussed. Lincoln, dressed handsomely, had the confidence of success and position. With Papa and Mama in the back of the buggy, and Abell, Anna, and Custer following behind, the family rode the short distance to the city train station.

"You all exit here, and I'll tie the horse," Lincoln thoughtfully offered.

The station had seen a hard season. Hundreds had passed

this way through the winter and it looked worn. Linnea asked Papa and Abell if they remembered when the old station was built, how they walked to town that day to see it opened with the fireworks and band.

"That was a good day," Papa recalled. "All the family together."

"A good day indeed," Abell agreed.

The chug of the locomotive sounded in the distance. It blew the whistle on approach.

"Where is Lincoln?" Linnea asked. "He is going to miss his parents' arrival."

Hsssssss, the steam poured out and across the planks as the brakes and friction screeched. William remained as peaceful as ever. The loud noises and new experiences bothered him little while sleeping in his mothers arms.

"Where could he be?" she asked again.

Passengers from the train started to disembark. First class passengers included dapper men, and women in big hats with bustles to match. Less extravagant men left the main cars with workers in the rear. The crowd filled the platform trying to move forward like cattle on the graze but with luggage.

"Linnea?" A woman called her name.

She turned to see the older, yet still familiar faces from Hillsdale that had been good to her all those years ago. "Hello? It's good to see you. What are you doing here?"

CHAPTER 37

"We're here to visit our son," Mrs. Baxter said.

The edges of Linnea lips dropped from the nervous smile to a flat frown from puzzlement.

"Our son, I mean, our son- his name is Lincoln. He moved here not two years ago and recently got married."

Linnea's mouth opened in surprise. Without a sound, a scream of fury and hell raged in her mind. A feeling of dread so large came over Linnea it felt like ten bales of straw fell at once. She couldn't breathe. She had never known a feeling this powerful before.

"Linnea, what's wrong, you look sick?" Mama asked.

"I thought you were in Hillsdale." Linnea shook her head in disbelief.

"We're in Lansing now. When you left, there was a bit of a kerfuffle on campus. Mr. Baxter took a new job after.

Campus politics, rumors, busy talk. We are more cautious now. The family even took my maiden name, Beaumont, for a fresh start in the academic community."

"Mother!" Lincoln joyfully exclaimed. "You found my wife and son."

A look of shock flashed across the face of Mrs. Baxter. Taking a step forward, leaning in, she eked out, "Linnea, what have you done?"

Linnea stood motionless, trapped between the families. She was paralyzed in trying to grasp the information. *Dear lord, what have I done?*

"Linnea!" Mrs. Baxter shouted. "What on God's good earth have you done?"

"Now, now, what's the trouble here?" Papa asked. "This can't be that bad."

"And who are you?" Mr. Baxter asked.

"I am Linneas father. Who are you?"

"Lincoln's father."

"It's good to meet you. Thank you for coming," Papa said. "Why are these two angry? I don't understand. This should be a happy time."

"Karlsson!" Mr. Olsen walked up the platform followed by this clan. "Is this the in-laws? Introduce me, as we'll soon be family."

"Linnea, do you want to explain?" Mrs. Baxter asked.

"I-I-"

"You're daughter," Mr. Baxter gulped, forcing the words, attempting to avoid being publicly sick, "had a child out of wedlock nineteen years ago."

"Wait," Linnea whispered, "no, stop, it's not like that."

"Linnea? Is this true?" Mama asked. "Not our Linnea."

Mr. Baxter pressed forward, "We adopted that boy and named him Lincoln." He pointed to Lincoln.

"I was adopted?" Lincoln asked.

A frenzy of questions began to pour out. Everyone looked to Linnea for answers. They repeated what they thought was said time and again. The whispers and mutters spread to each onlooker. The words and reality, the sentiment and truth merged in their minds. Everyone on the platform now began to understand what had occurred.

Shouting started from Mrs. Baxter, "Lincoln, you get on that train right this minute. We are taking you home." This was followed by Mr. Baxter, who grabbed his son's arm. Lincoln resisted, his arm struggled free, hitting Abell hard enough it knocked him to the ground. Anna went to Abell's aid immediately but tripped on the hoop of Mrs. Baxter's dress and fell over onto Abell.

Mama began to wail uncontrollably. She moaned loudly, repeating, "What did you do Linnea? What did you do?"

It was the cry from William that started to silence the crowd. The hush was a chill colder than anything the winter brought the last six months. It wasn't what Linnea had unknowingly done, but what they created as a result.

The whistle sounded. "All aboard" the conductor shouted for all to hear.

Hiram, watching from the postal car, stepped back inside.

Mrs. Baxter's voice, shrill and crisp, ordered, "Lincoln Beaumont, you get on that train this minute, young man!"

Instinctually, he did what his mother instructed. He was followed by his father. From under her big hat, Mrs. Baxter turned meeting Linnea in the eyes. Her parting words hung in the air for the city of Pontiac to hear, "Linnea Karlsson, you are a ratbag, blunderbuss and a wagtail! I hope you and that little *monster* in your arms get what you deserve!"

The good people on the platform watched in silence as the locomotive's big wheel spun on the rail and sand, catching friction on this second rotation, moving the long metal beast forward. A final sound of the whistle, the chug-chug-chug built momentum and speed, until the conductor with his green light passed them all, taking extra care to look at the woman who married her own illegitimate son and created a baby with him.

Linnea's heart raced as the planks underfoot creaked with the movement of the dispersing crowd. She was left holding William in front of her mother and father, brother and her soon to be in-laws.

Mr. Olsen broke the silence. "Anna, come."

She obeyed her father and followed her parents to their buckboard. Abell pursued as best he could, "Mr. Olsen, wait. Mr. Olsen, if I could explain."

"Mama? Papa?" Linnea pleaded. "Please, let me explain. Please."

The elderly couple who had been through every turn in

life together, surviving wars, plague, and starvation in the harshest conditions were left without words.

Linnea watched helplessly as her parents got into the buggy pulled by Custer and started to roll away. They stopped when Abell, alone, flagged them down to climb on board. Linnea was in tears, abandoned by her family and husband to care for William alone.

She allowed herself to cry for a moment more alone on the platform. Linnea took a deep and practical breath. Everything in her future could be parsed into the next series of steps. The logic from the math she learned, the books she read, bifurcated the world into a series of choices. It was a ninety-minute walk to her house. Maybe longer with the baby. Or, she could take the next ten minutes to find Lincoln's horse and buggy tied down the street. It would be difficult to hold the baby and drive, but she would manage. That was it. That was all she had to do. Think about the next step in solving the problem, not attempt to leap forward to the end. She would manage. Linnea made up her mind that she would manage.

The horse and buggy were tied on Pike Street. Passersby watched her with disgust as she searched for the correct buggy. People were whispering to one another, pointing at her with wide eyes. "I guess it's true, William." Linnea said. "Nothing travels faster than bad news."

Linnea focused on her task. She untied the horse, released the break, and picked up the reins. A leather strap in each arm, William cradled between the two arms and partially on her lap, she turned the rig to the street and slowly moved forward. Her buggy was passed by others going a normal pace, but speed wasn't her concern. Getting around the block and pointed in the right direction built confidence. She pulled over at the city line. Another buggy that might normally offer aid or inquiry, passed right on by.

Taking William's blanket she tied it into a cradle, like she had seen Indians do. Next, she tied it to herself. A baby pocket. With both hands free they moved at a normal pace and William was soon fast asleep.

Arriving home, she found the inside of the house a mess. Papa and Mama had beaten her home by at least an hour. They had used that time to remove their belongings to Papa's barn across the way.

With the horse tied, brushed, and fed, she marched over to her parent's barn. She started with a knock, "Papa. Talk to me, Papa. Let me explain." It turned into a pounding no one could ignore. Finally, he unlatched the door, blocking its entrance.

"Papa, please let me explain what happened at the textile in Detroit."

"I know how babies are made, Linnea. You don't have to explain."

"Then let me tell you the whole story, not what you've heard."

Papa's cold stare turned to a crooked face with tears. Linnea had never seen her father cry before. Not like this. This scared her more than anything. She felt that her father was honest and true only days before. His hope carried her. He would never stop loving her, no matter what. However, the salty tears and red face put this into question.

"You were supposed to be special," he said. "Our true American. You were going to be different. Mama and I talked for years of uprooting our family, getting to America. We wanted to give you things we could never have. You were supposed to be confident. You were going to find success. But all you did was find what we left behind in the homeland. You learned shame. The same shame we tried to leave in Sweden. Shame our family carried for generations. I thought we could improve our family's life by coming to America, finding a new station, and gaining respect in the community. But they will not forget. They will not forgive. That baby will always be a reminder of what you did, who you are, and the daughter we raised. We failed at being parents. You failed us with this shame."

"Papa."

"No. No 'Papa'." His voice was curt, cutting. "You leave. You have not learned your place in this world… and your place is not here. Not with me. Not with Mama. You go back to your house. The house you bought with the devil's gold. Think on your sins."

The high-pitch squeak from the metal rubbing metal of the hinge pierced the air as Papa closed the door. He had promised Mama for years to fix it, but never did.

1899

BOOK IV

1899

CHAPTER 38

$\mathcal{N}$early every wall in the house was covered by full shelves of books she had read and saved. The privately cultivated library would have impressed any professor. Used, discarded, reclaimed, or sample works that had value were on these walls. From the embers of the afternoon, she added three good sized dried logs and asked William to join her by the growing fire.

"Yes, mother?"

"Please, sit, join me. I want to speak with you a while."

William made his way to the high backed chair opposite her. He had spent his life growing into this chair, knowing every stain's story, the fit of the cushion perfectly matched his contour, each repair returning it to a solid state.

"Mother, what's on your mind?"

Linnea's hair, now gray, was wiry and under the control

of pins. In certain angles by firelight, she still had that spark people had found attractive since her youth. The tall collar of the blouse buttoned around her neck and the oxblood sweater layered over her shoulders kept her warm. The colorful afghan she made the summer William was four from the collection of penny remnants tied into granny squares lay across her legs, as it did three out of the four Michigan seasons.

"You've had many questions growing up, that I always answer with I will-"

"I'll tell you when you're older" William finished her sentence. "Yes mother, I am well aware."

"William, tomorrow, you will be eighteen. You are now older, a man. I've decided it's high time to answer some of your questions." She watched his expression change. "Is there a particular place you wanted to start?"

"Who was my father?"

"I thought you might start there. Your father's name was Lincoln, the son of a university professor."

"Yes, but who was he? How did you meet? Is he alive?"

"I don't know if he is alive. He left us shortly after you were born."

"Why did he leave us?"

"He was ashamed to be with me." Her eyes fixed on the fire's flame and watched it flicker. "The summer after he left, a lawyer knocked on the front door and informed me that our marriage was annulled. As I told you before, you are not a bastard. Those schoolyard boys are factually incorrect. I was satisfied with the annulment, as in his letter before that, he had considered putting me in the asylum where he was once employed, and you in the orphanage down the road from there"

"Did he hate us? He sounds cruel."

"No, he once loved us very much." Her declaration turned soft and wistful. "We were his everything. But you'll find in life, my dear William, that there are tough lessons we learn, especially about love. People often confuse love with lust. They are different things our bodies find similar but our minds misinterpret. However, you are going to find that love is both a feeling and a conscious decision. He felt love for us. I truly believe that. He decided it was best to leave us. And I agree. If he had stayed, things would have been different but not better."

William thought a hard moment, "May I ask you *anything*?"

"You may." She pulled the blanket closer. "But I may not give you an answer, or you may not like the one I give."

"The old couple, the ones that used to live across the way," he asked with caution, "why wouldn't they talk to me? Why chase me away at every chance? Why be mean? They would watch and stare at me. They couldn't take their eyes off me, but were cold and distant when I approached them. I was confused."

"They were my mother and father."

"What? They were family? I thought Uncle Abell was our only family."

"Abell was a good man, and a good brother. We remained close his entire life. I know you looked to him because he understood what it meant to face crippling adversity."

"Your parents? I can't believe that your parents would be cruel like that."

A crackle from the fire caught his attention as the bottom log burned through and broke in half from the weight of the other two on top. He stood and took the iron poker from the fireside to push the logs back and keep them from rolling apart.

"I called them Papa and Mama," Linnea continued. "They came from Sweden with my brothers, and I was born in America. Papa called me his true American for the longest time."

"What could have happened that would make them hate us? What could have possibly been so awful? "

"I brought shame to our family. And I have had a good amount of time to think on this, William, nearly your entire life. You see, there was a time when all the houses, all of our neighbors' homes around us, were actually farms and farm-land. My Papa owned all the land between the road and Mud Lake. I owned the back acres up to Paddock Road."

"You owned land?"

"I did. Your mother had an unconventional life. Before the city expanded and incorporated these properties there was a strong community of Swedes. Papa was a well respected man in the community. But the same year you were born, the people in the community discovered I had a child out of wedlock years before. That news, well, I brought shame to the family."

"Was, was I-?"

"No, not you. Your older brother, my first born. I gave him up to a loving family for adoption, and they took good care of him."

"I have a brother? I always wanted a brother."

"You do."

"Will I ever meet him? Get to know him?"

"No, I am sorry. I wouldn't know how or where to find him or the couple who took him in. It was long ago."

"Still, it's good to know I have a brother out in the world, maybe one day we will meet."

"Maybe." She sighed deeply hoping he never would. "What other questions?"

"My father-"

"William," she interrupted, "that time in my life, it was like a fevered dream that I woke up from with little recollection, and ugly images that terrified me. I wish I could tell you more."

"What did you do before being a librarian?"

"I kept the books for several businesses, like an accountant but without being bona fide."

"You would be good at that. You love math."

"I was good at that, and those first few years, as the library association formed, I still balanced books in the evenings. You were a good baby, and would come with me in the evenings, keeping busy while I did the books."

"It seems my entire childhood was in the library—all I remember is the library."

"Your love for reading was always a blessing. You would sit with a book all day given the chance, and still do."

"The man across the way, your Papa?"

"Yes, Papa."

"Abell said that he died from an accidental discharge of his gun."

"We told you that to protect you from the truth. He took his own life. When he died, Mama went to live with my brother Lars out west."

"You have a brother Lars?"

"I do, I have letters from him. He is a successful businessman in Independence, Missouri."

"When you said west, I thought he might be in California."

"West of Michigan. As a little girl, Michigan was the start of the west, and it took all day to get to Detroit by train."

"All day?"

"All day. When I was much younger, during the war, I took the train to Detroit and worked in a textile mill, while your uncles fought in the war. Except Lars, he went west. I think Abell would have liked to join him out west one day, but the shame prevented that."

"Why did the Olson boys taunt me? I've never done anything to them."

"The Olson boys' mother used to date your uncle Abell. Mr. Olson never liked that, because, well, I suspect that somewhere deep inside, Anna Olson still has feelings for Abell."

"Even as he's passed?"

"Even after he passed. Love tends to linger long after it makes any sense, William."

Linnea asked William if he remembered anything of the Christian Bible she asked him to read. It was a good six months he spent reading it through with the extended dictionary at his side. She asked him to remember the New Testament, and think of the apostles. These were examples of people who had strong faith, and often as people who lived a good or blessed life, following the words of Jesus.

"James, the brother of Jesus, was thrown from the top of a tower, then beaten to death at the bottom. The Apostle James, was beheaded by King Herold, and the only death mentioned explicitly. But when you look at the other apostles, in other texts, you'll find equally horrible and painful outcomes."

She went on to explain each. Matthew died by a sword wound in Ethiopia, Matthias had been stoned then beheaded. Mark in Alexandria was dragged by horses through the streets, and Luke hanged in Greece. Peter and Andrew were crucified after being beaten and whipped. Nathaniel, whipped and flayed. Thomas stabbed by a spear, and Jude struck down by arrows. The only one to die of old age was John, but that was after he survived being boiled alive and cast out of society to mine as a slave for decades.

"So, William, my dear son, in turning eighteen you are a

man. And you may pursue any life you choose. You could try to be a good man, and follow the fate of the apostles which came before you. But I would ask you to be your best as a man. Don't follow others blindly, and do better than what others say is good." Linnea pulled William into her arms, embraced him tightly. "No matter what you do, or find, I will always be your mother. I will always love you. There is nothing, and I do mean nothing, that you could ever do which will ever change that love I have for you."

After Williams' questions were satisfied, Linnea gave him the last present he might have for his birthday.

"When I sold the farm land behind our house and the land was developed into individual home lots, I set that money aside. It has been collecting interest this whole time. This morning, I withdrew the funds, and all this money is now yours. Three thousand, five hundred, and seventy-two dollars. I wish I had more to give you, but that is everything I have, aside from this house."

Williams' eyes grew large seeing the thick envelope and hearing the number.

"What have I always told you?"

"Courage lives on the other side of trying."

"It's time you seriously tried."

CHAPTER 39

The last kiss from mother, a last look as she waved good-bye, and William felt he should have been sad to leave her behind. Instead, the excitement and adventure of travel was flooding his veins.

After some time on the train and the second stop on the route, the scenery seemed less fascinating, the adventure still in the distance. Tree, tree, tree, bush, farm, building, building, building, seemed to repeat itself outside the window. He had seen bushes, trees and buildings. He wanted to see the city, the west, and cowboys.

A longer stop at the next station allowed him to stretch his legs. The cane his Uncle Abell had given him was a beautiful and sturdy sight with hand carvings. It gave a distinctive click in William's step that announced his approach. At the drag of his foot followed by a step and click, people would turn to see what made this distinctive noise. They found a young man with thick spectacles, thin hair, and pale skin. Always polite, he would touch the brim of his hat, or offer a tip of the hat with eye contact. William was never shy.

A voice from the train car asked clearly, "Are you William?"

He turned to see the old man in the postal car, behind the safety bars, out of the light.

"You are Linnea's son. I recognized the cane. It belonged to your Uncle Abell."

"I am he. And you, sir?"

"My name is Hiram, the postmaster for the line, and an old friend of your mother's."

"She never mentioned you, sir."

"It was some time ago."

With the call to board, William tipped his hat and turned to make his way back to his seat.

"William," the old man beckoned, "why don't you sit here with me, in the mail car. I will tell you about the first time your mother and I met." The door to the car rolled open. "It will be a rare treat. You can tell your friends about the time you spent in the mail car."

The white mail bag was more comfortable than the seat he had paid for up front. Once the train was in motion, the sway back and forth was relaxing, like a rocking chair at dusk.

"Linnea wasn't more than ten years old when she sat, same as you, on a mail sack headed to Detroit."

"Why?"

"Her father sold her to the textile factory, needed money in tough times. She wasn't the only one, but she was the first one I took. A hustler was hired to recruit cheap labor for the mill, something he did back east, I suppose. He worked the line and preyed on hard luck farmers. Last time I saw him was in Saginaw, where he was run out of town at gunpoint by the sheriff."

"It sounds like you've seen some things."

"Seen my share." He pointed to the faded scars on his face. "Detroit Labor Riots." He pulled up his pant leg to show a chunk of missing flesh "Robbery, 1878. Your mother is a good woman. She's smart, paid attention to her learning. She was beautiful, many men chased her, and she loved your father."

"You knew my father?"

"Saved his life during the Long Winter."

"What was he like?"

"Decent enough, but a fool to leave your mother. No offense."

"None taken. I only started to learn about him yesterday. Do you know where he is? If he's alive? Mother said she didn't know."

"Sorry, son," Hiram replied. "If your mother doesn't know, I sure don't. All I knows is, he worked up at the asylum a few years before he left Linnea and the baby. I mean you."

"That's what mother said." William watched Hiram sort mail. "Why do you think mother never mentioned you?"

"I asked her not to, asked her to leave me be. I was a fool to let her get away, too. Good lesson for you, William: don't let a good thing go."

Hiram removed an envelope from the small drawer of the sorting box, and started to write on the paper. In the same drawer he removed a stamp and pad. The official pound-pound from the pad to paper with the stamp seemed formal. He blew on the paper until satisfied it was dry, folded it in half, placed it in an envelope and handed it to William.

"What is it?"

"A free pass. You give that to any rail man, any postman, they will treat you good. That's my gift to you, William. Safe passage."

In Detroit, the two men shook hands before parting on their separate ways. William began to realize what his mother tried to explain. His mother had experienced a whole other life he had never known before the library. These last two days had been only a glimpse.

CHAPTER 40

*C*hecking in books was the last of the evening's chores before locking up. She reached for the top book from the stack, sliding across the wood worn smooth by a thousand other books, and opened the cover. Her stamp with the check-in date of the late spring of 1899 would go directly under the last.

Linnea opened the book in front of her, *Black Beauty* by Anna Sewell. She admired the first pages and noticed the book's loveliness in touch and feel. The hard red cover with the gold inlay invited the reader to discover what was inside each of the creamy pages. This book had been shared many times in the short ownership of the library. Some of the readers had left their mark: wear showed in the binding making it easy to open, and dogeared edges had been created by gravity after falling off a bed as the reader was lulled into a deep sleep and imaginative dream world. Many books held this grip on her library patrons, but none so quickly as this one.

Linnea read the first lines:

"The first place that I can well remember was a large pleasant meadow with a pond of clear water in it. Some shady trees leaned over it, and rushes and water-lilies grew at the deep end. Over the hedge on one side we looked into a plowed field, and on the other we looked over a gate at our master's house, which stood by the roadside; at the top of the meadow was a grove of fir trees, and at the bottom a running brook overhung by a steep bank."

That one passage from Anna Sewell transported her back to youth. It brought back the fond, yet sad, memories of her brothers, Horse, and warm summers on the farm as a child. When the ignorance of the rest of the world seemed perfect bliss, and there was the safety of the farm.

In reading this passage, Linnea remembered the reason she loved books, loved reading and math. For Linnea reading had been a safe way to fall in love without being ruined over the last seventeen years. Reading was both a way to remember and to forget.

Linnea looked up to see the thousands of books gathered here in one place. It was a small collection. The limited space of these walls, the basement, and attic still didn't equal much in comparison to what was available. For the curious mind it wouldn't be enough. The unquenchable thirst of knowledge had led readers away from this oasis to other fountains to feed them. This was how the world worked. She might help to shape it and spur the desire in some, yet the future was not there for her.

William was the future shaped from an unusual, and some might say unnatural, past. Linnea knew that William shared the right framework to learn and grow. A framework is a powerful start. A framework was all the Founding Fathers had for the constitution, and still this country was able to welcome the seeds to help it grow in new and different ways.

This was the best she could offer the world, giving William a chance for better choices.

PAPA ALWAYS RETURNED to Linnea in the fall, when the fields were golden, full of oats that sway and swirl with the warm autumn winds. From the snap of corn from the stalk, or the crunch of husks in hand, she could hear his voice tell her how to care for the harvest and when to reap. He was there in the winter when the split wood knocked together or the smell of the canvas lumber carrier started to warm inside by the fire. The thud of a hammer hitting the earth after twisting another nail, the slow gallop of a horse on the path, and when the smell of spring mud filled the air with a promise of an early thaw, she found him. Papa was with

Linnea always when the front door creaked a promise to be fixed.

She could see Papa in William walking ahead and looking back over his shoulder, urging her to keep pace. William carried his nose, and the edges of his eyes held the tender forgiveness of Papa's gaze she remembered when she had returned from the city to sit on the porch on long and lazy Sunday afternoons. And he was there always... always there when her boy became a man, when William's thick mustache tickled her face on each good night's kiss that wiggled like a fuzzy spring caterpillar.

This was life. She could see the distance from this height in years and looking back on all the events that had led her here. She knew that William would one day feel the same. Linnea wondered, *would it be the right spirits that haunt him?* He might remember her shush in the library when he had been too loud, the scent of older books she had saved, or the sound of cracking in the fire as mother and son read in their chairs at night.

Linnea was weary from her walk home. Each step and every corner was now haunted by people and choices made over the years. She felt weepy walking up the porch steps and decided to sit a spell instead of going inside to the lonely and now empty house. "Carpets, carpets, carpets," hushed off her lips as she allowed herself a moment to live in the past. Linnea could not seem to rise above the loneliness or find solace in solitude. Many evenings, like this one, she sat on this porch and watched across the way hoping to see a welcoming smile or a wink in her direction from the former residents. The road between them was unpassable, a barrier from forgiveness built with shame and shunning. What others had considered shame, she knew was hope. She had named him William.

The long nose and red friendly face of Mr. Fox III popped around the edge of the lilac bush. Still timid after years of visits following the introduction from his father, he sneaked up the steps and sat handsomely, wrapping his bushy tail around his feet.

"William is that hope," she said out loud.

The fox tilted his head with one ear perked in her direction.

"I suspect you are here for food."

The fox turned twice showing the delicate grace in his paws before taking his seat again.

"You can come in, but I don't have much to share, my friend. I saved one slice of jerk in the event you might visit." Standing from the porch chair there was a creak. She couldn't tell if it was the chair, the porch, or the weight of her life on her bones. "Come now. I have a letter to write."

CHAPTER 41

"*E*xcuse me, Lars Karlsson?"

The serious man turned, looking William up and down. "That's me."

Lars looked like a younger, more wily version of his brother Abell. Their broad shoulders, blonde hair, and barrel chest were nearly identical. However, Lars seemed earnest and humorless on first take, something one would never say of Abell.

"I'm your nephew, William Karlsson."

Lars took another look, seeing the cane, oversized boot, and thick glasses, "Linnea's boy? Your mother wrote to me."

"Yes. The very one." William waited for a reply, but when one didn't come, felt the need to explain. "Recently I've become aware that I have a family beyond my mother and your late brother Abell. Well, I was hoping to get more acquainted with the family, that's all."

After a long and uncomfortable silence, Lars replied, "You're a bit of a dandy for this life. But seeing as you're kin…"

"Thank you, Lars. I appreciate the opportunity."

"Where are you staying?"

"I have a room at the Friendly Lodger."

"Good, good, that's what I would have recommended." He took the pencil and pad from his smock to jot down the address. "Listen, I've got the business, but why don't you meet me at this address, family dinner, about 6 o'clock?" He handed William the note.

"Thank you, Lars. I appreciate it."

"I don't know how much you know about the family, but you should know that Mama lives with me and mine. She's not going to take kindly to you. So ya know. She has told us, that in no uncertain terms, would we ever talk about you or your mother."

"Yes, I've recently become aware of Mama. She lived across the way when I was a child. I look forward to finally meeting her."

"I don't know what happened, I don't want to know. All I ask is you go easy on the old girl. You're welcome tonight, but, ya know, if things go south, I'd ask ya to respect her and all."

"I believe I understand. This will be the opportunity I'd

hoped for, to know her, meet you, and in turn, would give you the chance to meet me also."

"Yeah," Lars rubbed his chin. "Well, we've both been warned."

———————

THE ANTICIPATION OF MEETING MAMA, a chance to talk with her and Lars to learn more about a family he had never known seemed too much. Sweaty palms curled to a fist knocked on the door. His heart raced like he was being chased by school bullies.

The large figure of Lars filled the doorframe, and behind him, nearly glowing by gas light, was an angelic figure.

"And this is my wife, Abigail, my daughters Adelaide and Emily, our youngest, my boy Vernon."

"A pleasure to meet you all. Thank you for inviting me to your lovely home."

In the moment of the handshake, William could feel the power and strength of his uncle. The squeeze was hard, skin rough, and the sinew between the thumb and forefinger tight like a cord. The slap on his shoulder nearly knocked William over, but he understood its intent was welcoming.

"Come in, sit down."

The click-step-drag of Williams gate caught Emily's attention, "William, what happened to your leg?"

An intake of air sucked at the mouths of every adult. This

question caused the same reaction each time a child was brave enough to ask something adults found impolite.

"I have a bad leg, Emily, nothing happened. I was born this way."

"Does it hurt?"

"No, no. It's the way things are. No pain, just different."

"I like your cane," the angelic Adelaide said. "Where did you find such a treasure?"

Taking a chair in the front room, William explained that it was crafted and used by their uncle Abell. He was the oldest of their father's brothers and had fought at Gettysburg as part of the Michigan 1st Cavalry, under Custer. He found the normal response to this story, eyes wide in amazement and a shift to the front edge of seats. William went on to tell about the cane's history, of the one legged, one armed, veteran's survival of the conflict and the careful craftsmanship over the six months when he taught himself to carve and shape this from a single branch of a 200-year old white oak that was split in two by lighting on the farm.

Captivated, the family hung to every word. They could imagine in the tale a heroic Swede fighting the confederates, and the self-rehabilitation to learn a craft after. The humor of a horse named Horse, and its successor a highly trained colt named Custer that took Abell on new adventures in the city named after the Indian Chief, Pontiac.

"You tell that story almost as well as Abell did," the old woman's voice rumbled from the other room. "Almost like you were there."

"I heard it many times," William replied. "I admired Abell."

"Mama, do you want to come in here and join us?" Lars asked.

"No, no," she pattered. Mama had become a dark storm cloud floating through the house thundering and flashing unexpectedly. "I am fine from here, thank you."

"How was your trip here?" Abigail asked.

"It was amazing. This was my first time going anywhere. Have any of you been to Chicago?"

Only Lars said yes while the others shook their heads.

"I could smell Chicago before seeing it. An icy fog off Lake Michigan had wrapped around the city and blocked any view. Stepping on the corner of Madison and Canal streets the pungent smell of rotten flesh and horse shit that made me wince."

The girls all laughed at the blunt language used only by their father.

"It was so dark out from the smoke and fog that carriages taking the line for new passengers still had lit lamps at mid morning. And the people, the throng of people on streets and boardwalks were simply astonishing. Suddenly, an explosion boomed behind me. Rattles of windows and thunder reverberated through the streets. It took a moment before I realized the source and made my way around the corner to the river. In my hurry, I noticed the people of this great city were unphased. They didn't take notice. Business was being conducted as usual. I carried onward in the direction of the white and gray plum lingering in the air and ash to find construction and the volume of effort of mankind before me to be amazing. Workers of all types with shovels and wheelbarrows hustled to the source of the explosion. Some had already started to dig, removing the rocks and debris. When I asked a stranger what this all was, he said," here William imitated the man's voice and accent, "'Dat der is the river project. Making it go t'other way, send all that crap to Saint Louis, where it belongs. Where you been, buddy? All dis noise been going on for years.'"

The room broke into laughter at his tale.

"I must say," he continued when the laughter subsided, "the metal machines seemed monstrous with the long necks of the crane scooping and guided by rope and cable. Ships, not barely twenty yards away from the blasted wall remained buoyed in the river with the wall of wood and earth holding the gusher back." William reflected for a moment. "This truly is a great age to be alive. We live in a wondrous world. And with a check of my watch, I made my way back to the station, not wanting to share the trip with salt or steers on the freight rail. I needed to join my trunk on the passenger line."

"What a grand story," Abigale said.

Adelaide's eyes were wide with wonder. "I could sit and listen to your stories all day."

"Why don't we adjourn to the dining room for dinner?" Abigale said.

On the way to the dining room, William came upon the

woman he knew was Mama. It was the most awkward moment. He smiled and started to introduce himself. Mama, arms folded in a chair by the window, gave a slight harumph. She looked the same as she had from across the road in his youth.

"Mama," he said, "it's good to see you. I hope you are joining us for dinner."

Her judgment covered him like the shadow from a grand tree in summer. Her presence loomed over him, chilly and dark. His only escape was to step away, back to the light and warmth of the rest of the family. He smiled and bowed awkwardly, then made his way to the dining room.

Lars was inspired by William's storytelling. In a factual, straight-forward sense, Lars explained the decision to move west instead of fighting the South. In a grab for land, thanks to the Homestead Act, he had been able to claim the full 160 acres. He and his team built dams and water locks for irrigation. Their camp turned into a house, which later turned into a ranch. After some time there was a fair offer from the railroad for half the north property, and a "wildcatter" from back east over paid for the south half and set about prospecting for oil. After the land was sold, Lars moved to Independence and built the Dock and Freight Shipping Company.

"How old are you now, Adelaide?"

"She's seventeen, as you well know, Lars," Abigale rolled her eyes at her husband.

"Well, that was all nineteen years ago when I met your mother, Adelaide. Next year is our twentieth."

"What amazing fortune," William replied. "What an amazing family you have. I am very fortunate to have spent this time with you."

All through the evening, he could feel the careful watch of Mama. From his chair, William would need to make an effort to see her while Lars told his story. Still, he could feel the burn of her stare. On the two occasions he was brave enough to peek in her direction, sure enough, those eyes were locked on him like a peregrine on prey.

When excused from the table, William was invited to the porch to sit a while while Lars attended some business, and Abigail saw to the kitchen and put the younger children to bed. This left the duty of entertaining their guest to Adelaide.

CHAPTER 42

"It certainly is a beautiful night. We can see clearly down to the Bryant house. I spent a whole summer watching them expand. It has twenty-one rooms! Twenty-one! Who needs that many?"

"It is lovely here. I've enjoyed my visit."

"I hope daddy didn't bore you with his stories."

"Not at all. I came to hear them. I hardly know anything about my family. I came here in hopes of learning more."

"Well, daddy has a few stories, but you got all the ones I know tonight. Mama doesn't talk about the past. Mostly she knits and sews. Twice a year she makes Semlor, which are delicious."

"Semlor?"

"You've never had it?"

"I can hardly say it."

"It's this incredibly soft bun. They are best when still warm from the oven. Inside is whipped cream she makes fresh, and she will sprinkle this light dusting of sugar on top. It is unbelievably good. I'm surprised she never made it for you."

"Well, she never spoke to me, except to chase me away from the street."

"I wonder why? Daddy said you and Linnea lived near them in Michigan."

"We did, across the street. Mother said that they stopped talking near the time I was born. That's about as much as I know. I was hoping on this trip your father, and Mama, might shed some light on these things. Or I might get to know my family."

Adelaide and William gently swayed on the porch swing in the late spring night. Pedestrians out for an evening walk waved or said hello. Adelaide seemed to know every passerby by name. William listened as Adelaide talked about her dreams for the future. In some ways, she reminded him of his mother: smart, ambitious, logical, and kind. Her mind needed to be challenged, and she hoped for an education. Adelaide feared that being the oldest, she might fall into the tradition of wife and mother before knowing what might be possible.

"No one has talked with me like this before," William said. "Especially someone as beautiful. Your kindness is foreign to me, and welcomed."

"Thank you, cousin. I hope this isn't the last time we

speak. Your stories and the way you tell them are compelling."

"I am an avid reader. Mother is a librarian, a book collector, and we have always enjoyed reading, sharing ideas, and discussions. You know, I don't believe I truly appreciated Mark Twain until I crossed the Mississippi or watched the Missouri from its river banks."

"I've taken the view for granted," she said.

"*Come live with me and be my love, And we will all the pleasures prove, That valleys, groves, hills, and fields, Woods, or steepy mountain yields.*"

"Oh, William, your words!"

"Not mine, Marlowes. Still, they are wonderful words."

Her hand on his was a gesture William had never known, the warmth and softness of her skin, the fragrance in the night air intoxicating, almost in a whisper, said, "No matter what happens William, promise me we will stay close. Promise me you will stay in my life, even if only in letters."

"I promise."

A sound was never so interruptive as a screen door slam.

"Adelaide, don't you think it's late?"

"Yes, Mama. It is late." Adelaide turned to hide her blush.

"Then you will say goodnight to your cousin, kiss your mother good night."

Adelaide stood, obedient and true, wishing William a good night and going inside with the same disruptive screen door slam. Mama, always the observant eye, watched her go out of sight into the house before sitting on the far porch chair.

In that moment, William wished that all doors squeaked like the ones back home. It was a preemptive notice that someone was on the way. The slam was an afterthought of having arrived and a startling thunder clap of being caught in the moment.

"So, you've come to learn about your family?"

"You were listening? It's true, Mama. I am curious. I don't know why some stopped speaking with one another while living across the way from each other for nearly two decades. How a daughter is not invited to her father's funeral and allowed to grieve. Why a child didn't know that the strangers across the street were in reality his grandparents."

"I didn't think you would have been old enough to remember."

"My mother hid her tears for a long time, that's what I remember. I attempted to introduce myself only to be chased away. This is my memory."

"You were walking in the street and sure to be struck by a horse or carriage."

William was unsure of himself or what to say, "It is obvious we have very different perspectives. You know the truth. You hold all the cards. I've come to ask if you might share them."

"She didn't tell you anything, did she? You may not want to know. You may later hate yourself for asking."

"Mother told me that she had a baby out of wedlock

before me, that she worked in the textile, after Papa sold her, or maybe rented her, I am not sure, that point wasn't clear. Then the truth evaporates like a puddle on a hot summer day. Something here is unspoken, or forgotten on purpose."

"What did she say about the house? The one where you were raised?"

"She explained her husband, Lincoln, left us shortly after I was born. There were threats to send my mother to the asylum, and I was to be sent to the orphanage. Instead, the marriage was annulled. She kept the house and land, eventually selling the land to investors."

The corners of Mama's lips curled up into a grin. He could see she had caught a big fish in this net.

"What? Please tell me."

"Your mother never owned the house or the land. It was always his. He sold the land to the investors, and allowed you and your mother to stay until you turned eighteen. When was that?"

"It's been two months since."

"Your father," she started.

"My father? My father, what?"

CHAPTER 43

"William, please open the door." Adelaide knocked again. "I know you are here."

William opened the door to his room at the Friendly Lodger. With the tip of his head and a welcome arm, he invited her inside.

"You're leaving? Already? I was starting to get to know my wonderful cousin, the storyteller, from the distant, magical land of Michigan."

William continued to pack his trunk while she watched.

"What is it? What could be that awful? What would Mama say to drive you away like this?"

"I am worried about my mother. If Mama is right, I fear the worst, that she may have given up."

"What did Mama say to upset you?"

"My mothers fear of being alone, or being abandoned,

would at times drive her mad. It's something she carried with her all her life."

"And now, she's alone?"

"She is."

"Did Mama say anything else?"

"She said that my father was an idiot and a fool. His mind was like a childs. My mother was so desperate from loneliness she married him without thinking."

"That does sound awful. But not like you."

Adelaide sat on the window bench that looked over the street. In the distance she could see the smokestack of a paddle boat on approach. The black trails from the engine floated up and away as it neared. It may be on the way to her fathers dock to unload and reload. There might be passengers. There might be goods. Guessing what it might be was always the fun part.

"I think I want to travel like you, William. The stories you've told, the sights, and people all seem much more interesting than Independence, Missouri."

"You should. If it's travel or education, it would be better to leave and find your own path in life. Your father made bold ventures to the west and found his fortune. I am sure you could convince him to allow you, or not. This is your life, you are responsible for your own fate. Try as they might, no one can do this for you. Be the true American, find and fulfill the promise made to Mama and Papa back in Sweden."

"What will you do? Where will you go?"

"I am going to return to my mother. Without a word from her, I am worried for her well being."

"Will I see you again, William?"

"Do you want to?"

"Yes. Very much. If it wasn't obvious from me coming to your hotel and knocking on your door at first light, yes."

William stood over Adelaide, and smiled. With the soft back of his fingers he grazed her cheek, in affection, "You have been good to me cousin. More than you might ever know. I've never known kindness like you've shown."

"Take me with you. Show me adventure, the world. You know that traveling unaccompanied will prove difficult for me."

William stepped back from surprise. He turned to his trunk and closed the lid, twisting the key to lock it, and placed the key in his pocket.

"I want to take you with me, Adelaide. I could think of nothing more enjoyable than your company. I am going to ring the porter, and go to the station. I will keep my promise to you and write. We are staying in each other's lives. I may return. If you still feel the same when I return, we will go adventuring."

The angelic glow from her reflection in the window, the smile of youthful joy and hope made William doubt he was the monster Mama had described. He would hide the truth from others. The shame in this family would end. How could something so lovely like his cousin want a monster?

CHAPTER 44

The front door of the house was unlocked. Each click and step across the front porch built up the speed in his heart in anticipation to see his mother again. It had been months. There were several adventures which bubbled inside him to share. Updates on her brother, a stark discussion with Mama, his cousin Adelaide, meeting Hiram —they would not be real in the world until he told these tales to her.

"Mother? What is this sign on the door about eviction?"

An odd, pungent odor struck him. Opening the door there was a familiar creek from the hinges he had missed. There was always an unkept promise to his mother to try and fix it, but she insisted on keeping it that way.

"Mother?" he called into the dark.

There was no fire to keep the house warm. Winter fabrics still partially blocked the windows.

"Mother?"

He ventured deeper inside. The smell grew stronger. He called out again. His heart now raced from the fear of her well-being, not from the excitement of seeing her again. Between the click and drag of his motion across the familiar wood floors, he could hear the whisper of a voice.

The ghostly white sheet on his mothers chair in front of the fireplace was in fact, his mother. Her deep sunken eyes open a slit, lips moving without a sound passing them, mouthing the name William.

He dropped his cane and knelt at her side, "Mother? What did you do? Mother?"

At his best speed, William was in the kitchen filling a glass with water, and back at her side. "Drink this, please, drink a little. Tell me what happened here? What happened to you? I haven't been gone for more than three months."

"William, my son." Her voice barely reached his ears.

His hand stroked her white hair. He could feel that she was cold. Looking at his hand, long strands of her locks carried in clumps with each passing.

William began to cry.

"Let me fetch a doctor. I will bring you some food. Please, mother, hold fast, don't give up."

"Done," she whispered, "finished."

As the last remaining evidence of life left her body, her final breath faded into the stillness, William let her limp body go. She was now resting in her favorite chair, by the fireplace, in her home.

The mix of sadness for his loss, the anger for her giving up, and uncertainty of what was next stirred between his head and heart. William opened the drapes fully to let light in the front room. It was nearly empty. All but one bookshelf was completely empty. In the fireplace he could see the cold reminder of book bindings and covers. In the light-filled kitchen he found only a few flakes of ground oats, not even enough to fill the belly of a mouse remaining. Every jar from the pantry, empty and licked clean.

He didn't need a doctor to tell him. From this evidence it was clear he caught Linnea in the last moments of life before she starved herself to death, having burned the last of her books to keep warm. On that day, when she gave him her life savings for his birthday, he only now realized she gave him everything. She hadn't kept anything for herself.

His loss and sadness welled up inside him and churned with the self loathing and hate he had felt growing up. He was the monster Mama described. A monster only a mother might love.

Struggling up the stairs, he found that no one had been up there for some time. Both his room and hers were empty of all belongings, likely sold for whatever few dollars she could get. Perhaps the true owner of the house, his father, had them removed as part of the eviction but couldn't bring himself to remove her.

Back on the main floor, William could hear the faintest

scratch at the back door. When he opened it found the two kind eyes on the red fur face of a fox. The fox did not recognize William and quickly turned and bolted off to hide in the yard. Seeing the sad state of the yard, with the long dead grass, and tangle of weeds where the garden and barn used to be, brought him back to tears.

An unopened envelope sat on William's chair across from his mother. He picked it up. His chair was the only place left to sit in the house. Facing her in front of the fireplace felt familiar. It was home. He wished she were alive, someone he could tell about Lars, Abigale, and Adelaide. He could tell her about Mama, and the stubborn sadness and regret she shared with him alone that night on the porch. It was too hard for Mama to see Linnea every day, so she moved. Always haunted by what could have been, what she could have done for her daughter differently, stopping her from going to the textile factory in Detroit. She would have rather starved looking back.

Some people talk of being a 'beautiful' corpse, the departed finally look at peace. Or that they simply went to sleep and never woke. William didn't think that true of his mother. In life she had a glow, a wit in her eye, and a vigor others wished they held. All of this was now gone. Her body, the vessel that held all the wonder, was now empty of that light and life. Her head looked like one of Mr. Edison's bulbs, the receding hairline enlarging the look of her forehead, curving down into her cheekbones, with a sharp angle to her pointed chin. The light was extinguished.

He opened the envelope to find a letter written in her hand.

Dearest William,

There is nothing left to be done. When you were born I promised to do anything to provide you a better life. You are my true American, perfect in every way, passing every test and struggle sent your way.

Mine was a lonely life, filled with mistakes, riddled with struggles others put before me. You were the one thing I loved completely. You are the best parts of me.

In the art of repairing broken objects, the Japanese will mend using gold as their resin. In this, to highlight the damage, they elevate the object believing that when something has suffered and carries damage, it also becomes more beautiful because of its history.

Your life repaired my heart, once broken, thought incapable of loving again.

Go, find something you love completely. Be better.

I love you, and always will.

Mother

His mind took him back to the day before he left. Her lesson in life from the apostles who lived a good life and died horrible deaths for a cause.

"Live your best life," she had said that day. He assumed she was giving motherly advice, but now he understood them to be her parting words.

There was another word from the far east that mother didn't mention, *Lingchi*. Death from a thousand cuts. If even part of the stories about her were true he understood the sadness that would last forever. Being sold to the textile mill as a girl, taken advantage of by adults, giving up a child to strangers, abandoned by a husband, shunned by family, threatened by the mad house, and left alone to raise a "monster" could drive anyone to self-destruction. Or like her beloved Papa, you might wonder on the taste of a shotgun barrel with your big toe poised on the trigger facing shame and a broken heart. At that moment William wondered how a monster might die or if monsters could only be killed by knights on a holy quest?

"You didn't think I would come back," he said. "Not with any life left in you. But I promise mother, I will live my best life for you."

William stood from the high back chair, gave his mothers forehead one last kiss, folded the letter and placed it in his pocket. With a push of the screen door he heard the unfulfilled promise of rusty squeak. He smiled to himself knowing that wherever he might go, that one noise would remind him, the best parts of his mothers life would be carried forward in him. There was a great big beautiful tomorrow just steps away from this front porch. One need only to take that first step to start. William was ready to see every bit of this world and stepped forward.

ABOUT THE AUTHOR

Paul Michael Peters is an American writer of thrillers, suspense, and the unexpected. He is best known for his twists and takes on the quirky tangents of life.

Broken Objects captures the spirit of America in the era between the start of the Civil War and the turn of the new century following the life of Linnea Karlsson, the first natu-rally-born American in an immigrant family from Sweden, now farming north of Detroit, Michigan.

Other works include the thriller *Combustible Punch*, which explores the psychological dance between that most unlikely of odd couples: a serial killer and a high school shooting survivor. Other works include *The Symmetry of Snowflakes, Insensible Loss,* and short story collections *Killing the Devil* and *Mr. Memory and Other Stories of Wonder*.

#paulmichaelpeters #thriller #suspense #unexpected

Follow him at:

- **Website**: https://www.paulmichaelpeters.com/
- **Bookbub**: https://www.bookbub.com/authors/ paul-michael-peters
- **Goodreads**: https://www.goodreads.com/author/ show/7077098.Paul_Michael_Peters
- **Facebook**: https://www.facebook.com/ authorpaulmichaelpeters
- **Instagram:** https://www.instagram.com/ paul_michael_peters/
- **Audible**: https://www.audible.com/author/Paul-Michael-Peters/B00CNRE6NU

COMBUSTIBLE PUNCH

Rick Philips isn't a fighter — but he is a survivor

Haunted by memories of a high school shooting, not even the bottle can wash away the gnawing guilt and creeping feelings of inadequacy that batter Rick's conscience daily.

His life has been a mess of broken marriages, writer's block, terrible choices, and the morbid pity of others. When he meets Harriet at a writer's conference, the record doesn't scratch as he falls back — only this time, he may not get up.

Harriet Bristol Wheeler is a dark temptress — and self-confessed serial killer

INSENSIBLE LOSS

If you had the chance to live forever, would you take it?

2053: An old man, Viktor Erikson, lies on his deathbed. Alone and with no known relatives, he is tended to by Olivia, a nurse. He has only one request: that she reads to him.

The request is not unusual, but the battered, leather-bound tome she must read is no ordinary book. Written in 1839, it chronicles the discovery of the fountain of youth by Morgana de la Motte – and Viktor Erikson.

What starts off as a swashbuckling adventure on the high seas in search of riches and eternal life soon transforms into something quite different: a clash between two personalities bound by love and deceit, locked together by a terrible burden of necessity.

What lengths would you go to – and what price would you pay?

THE SYMMETRY OF SNOWFLAKES

Hank Hanson's family is not only blended; it's pulverized by the weight of its own perfect symmetry.

To the casual outsider, Hank Hanson's life might seem idyllic. As a successful businessman on the verge of a major business deal and an all-around good guy, few get close enough to see the troubled soul underneath his open face.

The product of a family fractured many times over by his parents' multiple remarriages, Hank spends his Thanksgivings running a miserable, thankless gauntlet of visiting multiple family members.

One Thanksgiving, he takes an unscheduled detour and meets Erin Contee, a woman who might just be too good for him – but at the same time, perfect. As the two grow closer together, Hank believes he has finally found the missing piece in his fragmented life.

He has a beautiful girl, great friends, a business, and a family – so why does he feel so bad?

Mr. Memory and Other Stories of Wonder

Uttering the name Mr. Memory evokes the live performances and talk show appearances when he would impress the world with his abilities of recollection. His clarity of remembrance has kept listeners captivated for days while sharing the adventures of his life. In this collection of short stories, we learn the truth about Mr. Memory, the fantastic gone unseen, and a world of wonder which can inspire us to believe.

Subscribe to our newsletter for this free ebook.

Sign up with your email address to receive news and updates.

Made in the USA
Columbia, SC
19 March 2023

13803356R00150